Margaret Deland

Florida Days

Margaret Deland

Florida Days

ISBN/EAN: 9783337112752

Printed in Europe, USA, Canada, Australia, Japan

Cover: Foto ©Andreas Hilbeck / pixelio.de

More available books at **www.hansebooks.com**

FLORIDA DAYS

BY

MARGARET DELAND

AUTHOR OF JOHN WARD, PREACHER; THE OLD GARDEN
AND OTHER VERSES, ETC.

ILLUSTRATED BY

LOUIS K. HARLOW

BOSTON
LITTLE, BROWN, AND COMPANY
1889

University Press:
JOHN WILSON AND SON, CAMBRIDGE

TO

LORIN DELAND

May 12, 1889

PREFACE.

ONCE upon a time, very long ago, the *Traveller* about the world was careful to carry with him a Journal, leather-covered, and with brass tips upon the corners; not infrequently it was closed by a stout hasp and padlock, for the thought that by any chance a stranger might gaze upon his pages filled the modest *Traveller* with dismay. With this Diary open upon his knee, with careful quill, and with most delicate and precise penmanship, it was the habit of this Person (who was apt to refer to himself as the *Private Individual*) to note

his emotions as he gazed upon a mountain
flushed with dawn, or the gray stretch of
the breathing sea, or into the faces of men
so unhappy as to have been born in other
countries than his own.   To this he added
— scrupulous about an inch, and credit-
ing with careful courtesy his information
to the Verger — the height of the nave
of a cathedral, or the genealogy of a
Royal House, or any of those rumors
which commend themselves under the
name of History.   The Journal and a
mended pen gave ample opportunity for
graceful sentences, for moral reflections,
for intense self-consciousness, — called by
some the " Love of Approbation;" — for
was not each carefully written word to be
read by the tender eyes of those whom the
Traveller had left at home ?

We have seen such Diaries, all of us,
although very probably the writers jour-

neyed into an Unknown Country before we opened our eyes upon our well-known world. For the most part these dingy volumes lie in long untravelled trunks, — hair-covered, and studded with brass nail-heads, — which have been pushed under the dusty rafters of the garret. The Journals are preserved by force of habit, and with a decent regard for the Past; but no one ever reads them. All the world admits that the Journal is as obsolete as the *Private Individual* himself. Besides, the ink has faded, and the details and the platitudes are alike wearying. In fact, the Diaries belong to that *Once upon a Time* which was the age of the spinet and tambour-frame, the days of modest youth and travelling by stage-coach, — in a word, to Leisure and Good Manners. And more than this, they were written only for those who were left behind.

But to-day, no one is left behind;
every one has been everywhere and
seen everything, so that information is
as unnecessary as it is tiresome. Indeed,
the *Author* who under any amiable dis-
guise might venture to instruct, would be
instantly detected as an encumbrance, —
named occasionally in a less dignified
manner, — and when not received with
compassionate amusement (or ignored)
would find his well-meaning volume
labelled " *Guide-book*," and thrust upon
the dusty upper shelf of a book-shop.
Instruction, like an unused garment, has
become old-fashioned, and fallen into
wrinkles and decay. All is said, and
there is nothing new under the sun!

This admitted, what has the preface of
a book upon Florida to say? Only that
Artist and Author have no such threadbare
motive as information to excuse or to

commend their book. Instead, there has
been but the desire to bring the remembrance of emotions which were the Reader's own; to spread the yellow sunshine
before his dreaming eyes; to steep his
overwise insistent consciousness in a fog
of content; to gather a misty memory of
beautiful days, — to strike the key-note of
a harmony which each soul may fulfil.
So modest an object will not deserve the
ruffled protest of the *Learned Reader*.
His own remembrance is all that *Florida
Days* will venture to suggest.

M. D.

August 12, 1889.

CONTENTS.

——•——

The Town.

St. Augustine.

The Country.

Along the St. Johns.

LIST OF ILLUSTRATIONS.

•

THE TOWN.

FLORIDA DAYS.

THE TOWN.

DAYBREAK.

" Morn, in the white wake of the morning star,
    Came furrowing all the Orient into gold."

THE strip of water which lies between the
    island and the shore, is as gray at dawn
as the sky behind the orange-trees in the west.
It rises and falls with quick and heavy heaving,
like the bosom of a dreamer who is beginning,
reluctantly, to shake off the night in which he
has been steeped. Beyond, toward the East, is

the unbroken stretch of sea; and then, Europe
and Africa in the flood of day. Here, luminous darkness, and expectation. It lies so low,
this narrow heap of sand and shells, that from
a distance it seems but a higher ridge of the
gray water, except where the column of the light-
house rises like a cloudy pillar touched with
fire, and where a line of glistening white shows
that waves break along the level shore.

The island, set like a jewel in the murmuring
and waiting sea, is touched by the first gleam of
light; and the waves, lapping and folding upon
its shores, lift themselves up out of silence,
with the rising exhilaration of the dawn. The
tower of the light-house catches the earliest
hint of day; and the lamps, which have burned
with steady, cheerful blaze all night, grow pale,
and melt and flicker; — one hardly notices when
they go out altogether in the growing brightness, which holds a promise of violet and rose.
The shadows separate, and stretch themselves,
and loosen their grasp upon the low-growing
palmettos and Spanish bayonets, so that each
wet, shining leaf has a strange distinctness in

the gray air. The flush that spreads across the horizon, glimmers even on the bank of clouds in the west; the darkness and mist

unfold, like the petals of a mighty flower, revealing each instant, deeper and deeper secrets in its golden heart. Dawn sucks the flame of the morning star into itself, — a flake of light, sparkling, white and serene, then lost for very brightness! It is as though the star were itself the dawn, for no one sees it die. Then, from behind the curve of the world a rim of gold lifts and widens, and a quivering column of fire shoots up and down, — into the air, and into the water, which is as luminous as a green crystal.

That leap up of the sun is as glad as a child's laugh; it is as a renewal of the world's youth. The waves crowd and shout to welcome him as he comes stepping gloriously from crest to crest, across the sea. A spark, flashing through each curving hollow that beckons him along, lengthens and widens, until a golden path quivers from the horizon to the shore.

The moment of distinctness in the gray of dawn is lost; the island melts into a shining haze, — it is full day in an instant. Shafts of light wheel and sink into the waves; the world of sky and sea and far-off, low-lying shore is swallowed up in light; the round sun is no longer a distinct and golden ball, but has become the sky itself. And the spreading sea is one boundless flash and gleam, smiling and swinging, shining with a light which does not

seem to come from the sun, but from the
bosom of the air itself. The wonderful expanse of breathing, shimmering blue is broken
by lines of far-off waves,—so far off that one

only hears a murmur of that tumbling crash
of spray, which marks with changing curves
and circles, their gay advance upon the reefs
of shells.

These low white reefs have grown with the
ages. Perhaps each moment has its monument

in a shell so small and exquisitely frail that
the faintest pressure would grind it to dust;
yet, washed up in these ledges, and pounded
by the waves, and smothered by sand grinding
down into every crevice, the shells have been
cemented together until they have hardened
into a composite that is cut and quarried like
rock.   For miles along the island these ledges
run, crumbling beneath the fierce white fingers
of the waves, and then renewed again and again.

Coquina this shell-stone is called, and blocks
of it were hewed here once by convicts brought
from Spain.   One wonders if these fierce, unhappy men, working in chain-gangs, and ferry-
ing the sparkling heaps over to the
shore to grow into walls and
gateways and the great bas-

tions of the fort, ever saw that a vast and beautiful meaning might lie in broken human lives? How blank to the little creature in its tiny shell, which lived its short life with myriads like itself, were the purposes of those great currents in the depths of the sea that plucked its life away from it; yet, perhaps, no more meaningless than were his own sin and pain to the wicked man, toiling in blazing heat above the shell-banks on the island, with a ring and chain around his ankle and with a bitter heart. How could he tell the purpose of his broken life, or know that it might be needed in the path of that

> " Far-off divine event
> To which the whole creation moves ! "

The island, lying so low that from the opposite beach one can look across it to the reefs and breakers, was the safeguard of the town, sleeping tranquilly among its palms and oranges when it had need of protection. For the ledges and sand-bars extend far into the sea, like the fingers of an unseen hand waiting to clutch and crush the ships of any foe.

And how many foes there were! Indeed, that
narrow edge of flowers and trees, where the
shell-stone houses had been built, was continually importuned by men and elements. The
winds and waves assailed it from about the

northern end of the island, and it seemed a
hundred times as though it must yield to the
embrace of the entreating sea. Men, steering
triumphantly across the treacherous reefs, rav-
aged it with fire and sword again and again;
its beauty and its promise tempted every buc-

cancer who swept his glass across the low-lying
barrier of the island, where, to be sure, there was
a little watch-tower, on which a flag was to be
raised, to indicate the approach of pirates, and
allow the townspeople huddled on the shore
time enough to run away. Yet the island is
so flat that doubtless it was often the watch-
tower which first caught the keen eyes of the
outlook on those high pooped vessels with
swelling sails and straining masts. One can
hear the order of Sir Francis Drake to " put
about " that he might discover what this little
group of buildings could be, and so the " Golden
Hinde" was turned from her course for yet
heavier ladings of gold and spoil. No eye was
keener than Sir Francis's. Perhaps he prided
himself upon it, remembering how, on the
Isthmus, he had "climbed the goodlie and great
high tree," and gazed upon the Pacific, into
which he besought God that he " might sail
an English ship."

There is a curious charm about this dead
man, who was as free and brave and cruel as
his own ocean. His worn, brown face, as keen

and kind as the sun and wind together, showed
as little certainty of fair weather; but men
loved him.   A man of no justice, perhaps,

but of great generosity.   Indeed, there was a
certain frank cordiality about him even when
engaged in murder.   He was so full of joyousness — so free from anything like the mean-
ness of spite — that he would have taken it ill

had his victims felt a personal affront while his knife was at their throats. He seems to have grown drunk with glory and with blood: so did the passion for murder and for gain increase!

One falls to thinking how such a soul could occupy itself after a certain "sharp distemper" had brought him to that last day, when his one possession was a sail-cloth, weighted, and the only noise he could make in the world the splash into the swinging water at the ship's bows, — a bubble on the surface, and then the smooth and shining blue again. Surely he must have found it a weary thing to wake and find himself a naked soul in the gray silence of eternity!

The wooden watch-tower on the island went to pieces a hundred years ago, and a coquina light-house took its place; but not very long since, it, too, fell with an awful crash, in a great hurricane. It could no longer deny the entreating sea, which had plucked at its foundations for many a year, as though jealous that its own shells should resist it.

The Spanish bayonet grows thick among
the fallen walls; indeed, those glittering green
spears are brave enough to grow anywhere;
their tough roots tie them like twine to ledges

that overhang the water, or knot under the sand
until no spot is too shallow or too exposed
for them.   Even the white roads which wander
across the island are so encroached upon by
their sharp thorns that walking is not always
pleasant.

And that reminds one of the pleasure of imagination, as exemplified by the pages of a novel. For it is recorded that a man came from his hut "through a thicket of Spanish bayonets"! The possible and the impossible are not, apparently, the things with which a novelist need be concerned. Over on the shore these fierce and glistening leaves have been banished, and kindlier weeds have taken their

places along the roadsides, — although, indeed, there is nothing more stately than the spring into the sparkling air of the bayonet's flower-shaft, hung with white bells of blossom.

In the morning light the town stands clear and distinct; later, the golden gauze of noon folds it like a veil; but now the houses, crowding sociably along the narrow streets, with balconies that lean towards one another like the wrinkled foreheads of gossiping dames, are all clear and individual. With the young day there is an alertness of life, a keen joyousness,

that fades, as
the hours press
upon one another,
into the calmest
content.

Everything is white
and sparkling; the white
sand shines, the white
coquina walls gleam and
faintly glitter, the white
galleries with scarlet gerani-
ums and verbenas pushing out into the sunshine, have a look of absolute cleanliness and

sharpness of detail; but it is all a mood of the hour, and softens as the day grows.

Perhaps it lasts longer about the barracks than anywhere else: the uniform of the sentinel pacing up and down his beat beside the sea-wall, is so fresh and new; there is such a keen, clean smell of lime, for each possible stone and stump has its coat of whitewash; and everything about the place is in exact and cheerful order. There is an air of modern life here, of hurry and importance, which does not belong to the old town, and was surely never known inside these gray walls while the building was still a convent. But that time is very long past; it was given up to the garrison a little more than a hundred years ago.

One stops in the shadow of the doorway, to think of the prayers that were said here once, and of the consuming desire that once burned beneath the white silence of convent living. The desire was for salvation, truly, but it took the place of a thirst for gold or glory or love, and made Life; for one must desire something, to be alive: perhaps absolute satisfaction is only another name for Death. Here at least, in the sunshine by the sea-wall, there is an ebb of the soul's vitality, as the sleepy hours drift into noon, for one is content with mere existence.

The Missionary and the Adventurer had set foot on this golden soil together. Indeed, the Missionary would not have come had not the Adventurer proclaimed the way. It would be interesting to know whether the souls of those

saints in the convent were ever perplexed to
account for the necessity of the Adventurer,
with his love of gold and his cruel ambition, —
if they ever thought of that mysterious rooting
of good in evil which continually confuses the
mind and even drives it into contented sinning.

Sometimes, indeed, the Adventurer was so
good as to bring the Missionary with him.   It
was as chaplain to the " Illustrious Captain-Gen-
eral Pedro Menendes de Aviles" that Francisco
Lopez de Mendoza Grajales appeared in the
New World to cure men's souls.   Yet one can
easily see, in the sincere simplicity of his letters,
how truly he could sympathize with the real
object of the expedition.   He speaks of having
been offered a chaplaincy at Porto Rico, where
they had stopped for a time, " and," says he, " I
should have received a peso for every Mass said,
and I should have had plenty to do all the year
round.   But I feared to accept, lest I should be
talked about as the others were; and then, it is
not a city where one is likely to receive promo-
tion; and besides, I wanted to see if, by refusing a personal benefit for the love of Jesus, He

would grant me a greater, since it is my desire
to serve our Lord and His blessed Mother."

There have been many alterations in the
convent building during these years of soldier

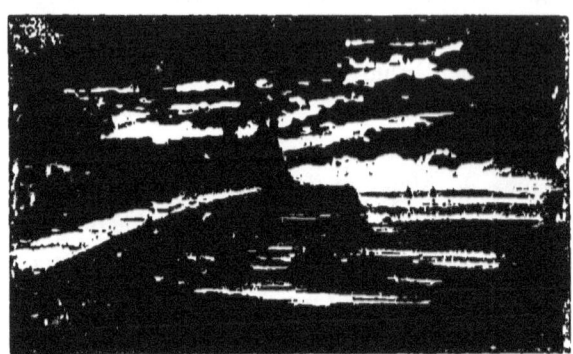

life, but the spell of the past is on it still. The
echo of a chant, the hint of incense, the murmur of a prayer for that bitter world of which
the petitioners knew so little, have a reality
of their own, although the outer ear catches
only the clatter of firearms and the careless
laughter of jolly fellows in the guard-room.

How those white souls who prayed in the

cells overlooking the sea would have shud-
dered, could they have guessed that instead of
the convent-bell at dawn there would be the
gay rattle of the reveille, and the tread of mar-
tial feet across the worn flags in the courtyard!
Very likely the world does not know whether
it is the better or the worse for the change;
the difference between a saint in the doorway,
reading a breviary, with placid down-dropped
eyes, and a sleepy boy, with a musket across
his shoulder, pacing up and down beside the
sea-wall, is not great enough for choice. Yet
who will measure the force of that thin, high
spirituality which once filled these walls, or
say that the boy himself is not the better for
prayers he never said? His rollicking song
when off duty has surely an unheard refrain!

We are shut in by mystery when we would
follow the flight of wonder from the safety of
our ark of commonplace. They were wiser,
those saints. They amused themselves with
dreams of heaven which, having always a like-
ness to the well-known and familiar face of
earth, brought no confusion and perplexity with

them. Yet even such simple dreams have some
disadvantages; with continual looking forward
life must have become merely expectation, and
a spurning of the present, — although that is
the lot of most, whether heaven is the name
of the future or not!

The past and the present and the desired future must have been very much alike to these
long-dead saints. Few of them could have had
anything but aspirations upon which to medi-
tate; for what lapse from virtue was possible
within these sacred walls, except, perhaps, reflection upon some sin committed when in the
world, for which penance has been done long
since, with great humiliation and fear?

It is curious, however, how much pleasure
comes sometimes with such a reflection! Indeed,
in a wicked way, it is an incentive to good living
to observe the spice of enjoyment there is to a
godly soul in a very little sin. Some small and
selfish pleasure, perhaps; a worldly book read,
breathless, with frowning brows or disapproving
murmur; — a criticism, maybe, of a holy thing;
— what excitement in such proximity to the

Devil! A good woman once said that Jacob
— her voice was lowered a little — *Jacob was
mean!* This hanging upon the edge of Biblical
criticism, this venturing an opinion of her own,
had the flavor of atheism ; but it was delightful.

They visited the sick and dying, the good
nuns, and they had their embroidery, and the
excitement of confession ; often searching the
soul, no doubt, for some possible sin, — for any
sharp temptation or tearing grief cannot be imagined within these placid walls. One wonders
if there was any slightest difference between
confession to the mother superior and the good
priest who said Mass in the chapel.

There are two passions of the soul which
are so much alike that they shade impercep-
tibly into each other ; it must have been hard
for the sincerest Penitent to know her own
motives in choosing who should absolve her.
Spenser says : —

> " Sweet saint, it is no sin or blame
> To love a man of virtuous name ! "

A little sophistry like that would make it all
seem right, surely.

Placid living brought length of days. The dates of the coming and the going upon some of the wooden crosses in the burial-ground are very far apart. " Sœur Marie: Requiescat in pace. Joseph: Marie: Jesu; " and then, perhaps, seventy years or longer.

How many years of vacancy that must mean for Sœur Marie, if she became "religieuse" at twenty! One falls to speculating upon the crisis of those twenty years, — the possible catastrophe which made life seem worthless, or, perhaps it were truer to say, made the preparation for that other life seem better. If the end — these fifty years — was Religion, surely the beginning was Love! It is safe to infer as much as that; and how often in these fifty empty, tranquil, waiting years may not Sister Marie have lived over again the pleasure and the pain that drove her for relief into silence, — silence which had no sorrow and no disappointment; only the precious memory of a disappointment, which for all its pain she would not lose even though she did penance with every prayer!

The memory, perhaps, of a look from be-
l jalousies; a fan held sideways across a
cheek; a kiss, maybe, in the fragrant dusk
'neath a blossoming orange-tree;—fifty years
i penitence will atone for a kiss beyond a
ibt, but one cannot be so sure of the fan;
t is a far deeper evil than anything so nat-
.l as a kiss! Between that very human and
iple impulse, and the flutter of a fan, the
. rence is the difference between a sin of
heart and a sin of the head; the former is
.d'y a sin at all, the latter is deliberate and
ational. There is the look across the white
.hers, the fingers trembling on the ivory
ks, there is the politic weighing of the
. rver's heart, the calculating with greatest
. 'y upon his emotions. Steele said that the
.wounded more men than Cupid's bow;
I s cle's opportunities for observation can-
b questioned. And there is another ac-
l d_ment of its power which makes one
d' f his "Spectator," although its source
i lover one. "A Spanish lady with her
. h hame the tactics of a troop of horse,"

it declares. "Now
she unfurls it with
the slow pride and
conscious elegance

of the bird of Juno; now
she flutters it with all the
languor of a listless beauty, now with all the
liveliness of a vivacious one. Now in the midst
of a very tornado she closes it with a whir

which makes you start. . . . Gallantry requires
no other mode to express its most subtle con-
ceits or its most unreasonable demands than
this delicate machine."

So it would appear, then, that Sœur Marie
may have had need of repentance; but fifty
years is a long time!

The old Cathedral on the Plaza, where very
likely the breath of a fan has blown the sermon
from a man's memory a hundred times, was
burned not long ago, but the new one has re-
produced it with a tender fidelity to the past.
It, too, faces the Plaza and the old market, and
the monument that the Spaniards raised just
before they took their departure from the town.
The morning light strikes it fresh and clear
from across the live-oak trees in the square, and
through the palmetto leaves in the garden opposite it. The old bell which the flames spared,
on in the new belfry. "Sancte," its inscription runs, "Sancte Joseph, ora pro nobis.
D̃ . . ." It was brought from some Spanish
only a century ago, when the old Cathe-

dral was built, and had doubtless traditions and
memories of its own, before it began to ring in
the joys and sorrows of
these hundred years to the
sleepy town. One fancies
it marking, in its gray
belfry shades, the con-
tradictions of human life
which have danced and
burst like bubbles
on the surface of
these two hun-
dred years. A

hand upon the bell-rope, and it
has clanged joyously for the vic-
tory of an invader, and again as gayly
for his defeat. It has pealed for a king's life,

4

which meant another king's death; it has rung
for birth and burial, for famine and plenty.
And then, the rope dropping into a careless
coil from the ringer's hand, it has thrilled and
sung with wonderful unseen vibration, telling
over to itself, perhaps, its own thoughts. There
is something about this sibilant whisper of a
bell, after it has done man's bidding and he
has left it, which is as though it spoke its
own mind in silent laughter at his little joys
or griefs.

The Plaza and the market-place beyond have
often answered its call for this thing or for that.
No doubt it summoned the loyal subjects of
King George to burn Hancock and Jefferson in
effigy just as loudly as it has called for flags
and music each fourth morning in July ever
since. It has watched the people coming out
from early Mass to their day's work in the
Market, to chatter and cheat, — the more com-
fortably, perhaps, because prayers have been
duly said; and from its perch beneath the
golden cross, it has seen the soldiers manœu-
vring in the Plaza, sometimes with all the re-

ality of war, and again with light-hearted
imitation of earnestness. It has rung, too, for
that strange gayety of Good Friday night,—
the reaction from the forty days of darkness,
which wore the guise of devotion.

For to shoot at straw figures decked with
feathers and tinsel was a spiritual exercise,
when one called the effigies *Jews*. So, with
light-hearted laughter, as night fell, the Jews
were hung here and there in the Plaza, under
the live-oak trees or upon the lamp-posts, so
that when morning dawned there might be no

time lost in proving who was the best marks-
man and the most devoted Christian. For very
many years this was the custom upon that Sat-
urday which lies between a dark day and a
shining day, that pause between death and life,
while the dead Christ waited in the Cathedral.

On Easter eve the joyousness began again,
and young men went about the city singing
the story of Jesus and the Resurrection. The
musical Spanish and the starlight were worship in themselves. The singers knew the
words by heart; so who stopped to wonder,
or to search for deeper meaning in them?

> "Let us leave off mourning," —

so the English runs, —

> " Let us sing with joy.
> Let us go and give
> Our salutation to Mary.
>   O Mary !

> " And at midnight
> She gave birth to a child,
> The infinite God,
> In a stable.
> At mid-day

> The angels go singing
> Peace and abundance.
> And glory to God alone,
> O Mary!"

And so on, through that Story which belongs
to all the ages: of Birth and Death, and of
that inevitable morning, which came to the
dead Christ, even as it comes always, upon
the heels of Death, with a meaning which Eternity can only blur, and toward which all Time
has travelled. That solemn "day after he has
died," when a man's life stands naked, without hope or illusion to make it beautiful; —
the empty days have not come yet to stand,
pitifully, between Truth and Love; — even
those fisher-folk in Galilee saw that morning!
Perhaps the necessity of the world found
its expression because of their misery that
day.

And it is because of that necessity that
the young men, with flowers in their hands,
went about through the streets and in the Plaza,
singing in the starlight of the glory of the
Resurrection!

The singers could buy their flowers in the
market, which is but a little way from the
Cathedral. Whitewashed pillars uphold its
ancient roof, and its brick floor is so old that
it is worn into hollows; it used to be filled
with stalls, where great heaps of vegetables
and yellow oranges were displayed for sale, or
where the wet sides of fish sparkled on every
scale with wonderful color. There were sun-
bonneted women gossiping in the sunshine
across their wares; men smoking under the
streamers of moss from the live-oak trees, or
chaffering over their mules and horses; — a
crowding, good-natured, quick-tempered people, bringing color and laughter into the little
square; they came for the most part from the
country beyond, along the shining shell-road
and through the city gates.

As long ago as the beginning of this century
the towers of the gateway in the wall about the
town were crumbling and broken with age, so
that they must have witnessed many things
unknown to the tranquil life which comes and

goes under their gray shadows to-day. They
see nothing more startling now than lovers
whispering in the twilight, perhaps; or the

gay tramp of marching feet which have never
known the hurry and terror of war; or a sob
beside a funeral bier.

True, Love and Death, — there could have
been nothing more ultimate than they; but
the expression changes; and these square

pillars crumbling slowly in the white, hot sunshine, have seen quick and nervous lives and
cruel deaths. The iron gates which used to
hang between the two coquina towers were
always closed at night, and fastened with pon-
derous bolts, so that the little town might
sleep peacefully within them.   How many

enemies of the King of Spain they have re-
pulsed when the town was garrisoned by his
soldiers, and how often they have received
and sheltered terror-stricken wretches flying
from the outlaws of the plains beyond!

A darky goes jolting through now, in a little
two-wheeled cart, full of yellow oranges. He
sings, perhaps, in a full sweet voice, but with a

certain wild note in it, which it will take many
generations yet to tame. " Oh, my Lawd," he
says, leaning forward, his elbows resting on
his ragged knees, and the reins slipping carelessly between his fingers, —

> " Oh, my Lawd, don't you forgit me,
>   Oh, my Lawd, don't you forgit me,
>   Oh, my Lawd, don't you forgit me,
>   Down by Bab'lon's stream ! "

With this morning freshness in the sparkling
air, he sings because he cannot help it; — long
ago the Lord remembered the captivity in
Babylon, — but the song has found no deeper
meaning in his soul; it is only a simple rejoicing in the sunshine. It is hard to realize,
in the comfortable content among the negroes,
living tranquil, sleepy lives in the old town,
that these words were ever sung with tears
and prayers; such pain meant alertness and
eager life, for which one looks now, for the
most part, in vain. These people would surely
never rouse themselves to contradict the man
who asserted, with grim disdain of all intense
life, that the happiest moment each day, to the

happiest person, was the moment when consciousness began to melt into sleep.

A woman, sitting in the sun with half-shut eyes, her pipe gone out perhaps, her head resting against the door-post, is quite satisfied and happy. She would be the first to say that these days of peace and sleep were better than

the old desire and the quicker thought. It has seemed to be either one extreme or the other with them, — the goad of pain, — and activity; or the down of comfort, — and dreams.

The boy in the jolting car, even though he sings, is half asleep. He apostrophizes his mule, or the oranges which tumble about his feet, with violence of words, but with a face full of lazy good-nature; indeed, he and his beast have the same placid way of taking life. The mule does not mark his abusive entreaties to proceed, any more than the boy notices or objects when his gray friend comes to a halt, and, turning slowly in the broken, rope-mended harness,

bites at a fly upon his shaggy side. But who shall dogmatize on such an attitude of the mind? Indifference, after all, may be height instead of depth. Does not "*A. B.*" (his modesty has given us no more than his initials) write as long ago as 1595, in "The Noblenesse of the Asse; a work rare, learned, and excellent," of that characteristic and admirable calm? — "He [the asse] refuseth no burden; he goeth whither he is sent without any contradiction; he lifts not his foot against any one; he bytes not; if strokes be given him, he careth not for them." A. B.'s honest appreciation of this patient and respectable animal leads him yet a little further. Their "goodly, sweet, and continual braying," he says; and adds that such brayings "forme a melodious and proportionate kinde of musicke." Still, all this is but the small adornment of an estimable character; the great thing is his beast's "tranquil calm."

"In the afternoon they came into a land
In which it seemed always afternoon.
All round the coast the languid air did swoon,
Breathing like one that hath a weary dream."

A DATE-PALM,
leaning across a
fence that is gray
with lichen, looks down
into the silent street, which

seems in the blaze of sunshine to be sunk in
sleep. The flood of light laps and ripples
against crumbling walls. A man with a lean
dog at his heels passes with noiseless foot-
steps, like a shape in a dream. A woman,
leaning from the upper window of a house
beside the sea-wall, laughs, and a spark of
sunshine flashes from the gold cross swinging
at her brown, warm throat, and then dims and
fades in the overpowering brightness; her voice,
which seems to have dropped through golden
distances, melts into the flowering silence of
the hot noon. The heavy sweetness of distant
orange orchards has, without a breath of wind,
invaded the old town; it makes the air, which
is the very light itself, a subtle caress; and it
brings a deeper dreaming, and a greater content
with Life and Love and Death: they seem
all one in this flood of ineffable shining.

The point at which each experience touches
the current of Life and claims personality, is
strangely blurred and smoothed. The individual
sinks into the mighty stream, and his consciousness is only the sunshine itself, and the air, and

5

light, with, perhaps, the same rejoicing in them
all that the date-palm has, or the gray fence,
crumbling under the tufts of lichen.

To lean back against the coquina wall, which
glitters here and there, as the sun strikes the
edge of an iridescent wonder, which meant life
in the green stillness of the sea a thousand
years ago; to feel, and to desire to feel, of no
more importance in the universe than a block
in the broken wall, or the motionless shadow
of the date-palm, lying like a gray feather upon
the dust of the dreaming street, — is good
for the soul. Experiences begin to show their
values relatively, and the proportions of life
reveal themselves. But it needs the coquina
wall gleaming faintly in the sunshine, and the
breath of the drowsy air, and the shadow of the
palm, to set the jarring atom of consciousness
back into the tranquil and enfolding purpose of
Eternity. Such an hour is the man's Bo-tree.
In it, truly, he gains the whole world, if he can
      his own soul.

It is extraordinary what a shame (not a passionate and tumultuous shame, — that were not

worth while, — but what a slow and placid shame) fills the dreamer against the wall, that there should ever have been any anxiety or wonder or grief in life. What arrogance to wonder! What folly to grieve! It is all as it should be, somehow and somewhere. It is not worth while to question how and where. A leaf from the vine hanging over the wall drifts down through the still heat: as well that it should set itself to question the currents of the ocean, lying in a blue and shimmering curve against a sky which is pale with light. No, it is not worth while; nothing is worth while, and yet all things are.

Gardens sleep behind these high walls, which shut them in so closely from the silent street, that it seems as though the air never stirs under the shadows of the oranges and oleanders. The only movement is the thread of water, trickling from the mossy basin of the fountain in the centre, and then losing itself in the deep grass; though if a sunbeam through the roof of leaves strikes it, it has one sparkling instant of jewelled

light before it fades into green dusk again.
The grass is thick in the wet darkness along
the walls under the tangle of jessamine; and
springing superbly out of the shadows at its
feet, a great palm will lift its stately head into
the dazzling sky.

Such a garden is very still; the jessamine on
the wall holds the brimming light unspilled in its
gold chalice; a petal from a rose's open bosom
floats rather than falls in the stagnant air, although, up above, the palm-branches swing and
whisper, rustling faintly in a wind which is not felt
below. Heavy-headed roses make the air faint
with sweetness, and orange-trees, thick with blos-

soms, drop white petals on the worn, wet bricks
of the path; all is very silent, drunk with sun and
air and perfume.   There is no thought, no ten-
sion, no meaning, anywhere.   A wooden bench,
painted green very long ago, has crumbled and
rotted, and breaking in the middle fallen down
into the deep grass.   A single shaft of sunshine
threading the shadows, strikes hot upon a line
of rusted nail-heads that hold it to the support-
ing post beneath; and there a lizard, bright-
eyed, alert, lies like a scarlet thread.   A cloud
of midges circle above the fallen blossoms of the
orange-tree, which are floating in the clear, dark
water in the stone basin.   The years have left
no more permanent life here than the dancing
midge, or the white cup of a fallen flower!

There is an empty wicker cage under the
hanging balcony of one of the deserted houses
about which such gardens lie; but the bird
must have flown away a score of years ago, and
not even a hint of its grief and its captivity
remains, for a scarlet tanager balances gayly
upon the swinging door before it darts like a
winged flame up into the blue.

Nature knows no sentiment. Her weeds and grasses come boldly up between the broken planks of the porch, with a joyousness which is almost insolent. A Cherokee rose lifts its silver shield in the doorway, and a tangle of blossoming briers chokes one narrow window and pushes between the fallen weather-boards. Indeed, so many weather-boards have loosened and fallen, that there is an entrance at more than one place; and the door, too, stands open. Strangely enough, a rusted key hangs still beneath the lintel, as though to guard a threshold over which the lizard glides, and shadows come and go.

The wall upon the street is of coquina. The windows in it have been boarded up, for sill and sash have long since vanished, so readily does wood crumble in the hot, wet shadows; but even these shutters have warped and broken, so that the passer-by can peer into the dusky room within. Its hard earthen floor is spotted with a dim, white mould; there is no furniture except some empty shelves upon the wall, and a crucifix over the narrow mantel, which is only a projecting ledge of the shell-

stone chimney-piece that encloses the wide, black fireplace. But beyond, through the sagging doorway, is the green light of the garden, and the palm-tree swinging against the low blue of the dazzling sky. Deserted and given up to Nature's careless triumph, the house has still the mystery which makes a dead body sacred: it has sheltered Love and Hope, — although the tiny shell in the wall has had more immortality than they.

Some of these deserted houses in the old town, set back in neglected gardens, behind smart new buildings, are still homes in some sort, in that they can offer a slight shelter from the kindly sky to any forlorn and homeless wanderers who, like themselves, have lost the meaning of living, but who still exist. Almost all hold a bed, and a bit of looking-glass stuck edgewise into a chink in the wall, thus providing for the two parts of life, — consciousness of self, and a safe forgetting.

The "King's Forge," near the sea-wall, has these two things, and a chair or two beside, and a tin cup and platter on a shelf. The walls

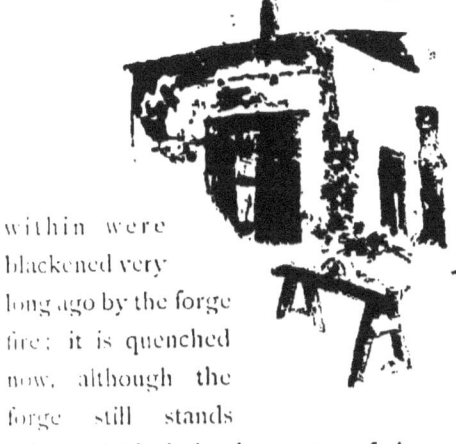

within were
blackened very
long ago by the forge
fire; it is quenched
now, although the
forge still stands
grim and black in the centre of the room, and
answers the purpose of table or shelf. The roof
is heavy with years, and has bent and broken,
so that a finger of light, thrusting itself between
the warped gray shingles, points down into
the dusk of the room, and moves, as the day
moves, across the earthen floor and up the opposite wall. It is so distinct, this bar of sunshine, that a mote can be seen, coming into it
from one side of the clear darkness through
which it falls, dancing across it, and vanishing

again into the dark. The moving spot of gold touches perhaps a hammer, dropping from its broken handle, a ring in the wall where a horse has been fastened, or a blacksmith's apron hanging high upon the chimney breast. That plummet-line of Noon gives the darkened room mysterious possibilities; it sounds the Past. It is easy to remember, or at least to imagine, in this silence, clamorous with dead sounds. One hears the hoarse wheeze of the bellows, or the champ of bits and pounding hoofs, and the blow of a brawny hand upon a steaming flank.

"Dey do say," — there is a hut beside the forge, and in the open doorway a wrinkled, grizzled negro is sitting in a broken chair, with a corn-cob pipe between his lips (it is he who plays the host with neighborly kindness for the absent owner), — "dey do say dat dey all comes back ag'in; do' I ain't seen 'em, dat's a fac'. But an ol' lady, an ol' cullud lady, dat lib in dere all by herse'f, she *say* she seen 'em many and many a time. Say she seen de horses prancin', and soldiers swearin' and singin' songs, and de black-smif orderin' 'em roun', — 'Sho! Git over dar! Whoa, now!' Dat's what she *say*. She's gone now herse'f — *somewhar*, so prob'ly she knows how dey gits back. She'll be right glad to know dat, she was allus so cur'ous. And she'll fin' out all dere is to fin' out! She used to say she like to know how dey clo's lasted, — her clo's did n't last, for sho'. She was disgraceful ragged!"

The man observed his own tattered sleeve with complacency.

"Well, fur me, I don't say nuffin' 'bout ghosts, one way or de oder. I don' know nuffin', — dat's a fac', — dat dere is any, or dat dere ain't any. If I said dere is, I'd be scar't; and if I said dere is n't, den dey might be 'fended. So I don't say nuffin'. Well, yes, to look roun' and see how it's over wif 'em whedder dey comes back or not, do make life seem mighty singular hort. Yes, it do. But dere's a pow'ful lot o' trouble in it, fur its size! Dere was a time when I was n't right sho' in my mind whedder it was all *wuf while*, — all de trouble, just for de sake of eatin' and drinkin'. An' I 've had my share o' trouble, so I tell you. I loss my fust wife, and I loss my second wife (cos', dey bof died happy); den I loss my modder, *she* died shout-in'! But a modder's not de same as a wife, — you can't *git* anodder. Well, an' money come hard, an' it seem like as if you was always want-in' just a *leetle* more o' suthin'. Always wantin'; — dat 's my sper'ence. De only peace o' my mind, when I come to think it over, was when I was asleep, or settin' in de sun, wif my eyes shut. Well, I thought it all over, and *den* I 'flected. I 'flected dat ef you had de Lawd, it *was* wuf while; and ef you did n't have de Lawd, den it *was n't* wuf while."

A clean, high soul, too wide to dare to limit Infinity by a word, said something strangely like this, once. "I see," he said, — " I see that when souls reach a certain clearness of percep-tion, they accept a knowledge and motive above selfishness. A breath of will blows eternally through the universe of souls in the direction of the Right and Necessary. It is the air which all intellects inhale and exhale, and it is the

wind which blows the worlds into order and
orbit."

Here is the conclusion of the old negro, sitting with vacant face in the sunshine, in the
crumbling doorway of the " King's Forge." He
might not recognize his own thought in the
broader words ; yet it is there. But if it is
worth while, it is a pity to bear it in a mist of
dreams; and this flood of noon blurs a man's
thought, as the opiate fragrance of incense dims
the aisles of a cathedral. Although, indeed, the
soul is often too content with sleep even to
desire a dream simply not to know, and, therefore, not to care, or to suffer,—that seems to
be the wisest thing in life.

A white pigeon circles slowly through the
placid blue depths above, round and round,
until the eye ceases to follow it, and only sees,
vaguely, a flash of silver coming and going, that
soothes like the murmur of a song above a
cradle. The rippling coo from milky-white
throats of pigeons, swaying and balancing on
the shelf of the cote, the soft gray of their wings
touched with iridescent gleams ; the slow swing

of great banana leaves against the sky; the lazy
splash of an oar beyond the hot sea-wall, — are
all parts of a stupor from which one would not
be aroused. Perhaps, if it were not so still in
the blaze of light, if there were any sound except that distant splash and the murmur of the
pigeons, it would be easier to awake, and once
more wonder and desire and feel them both
worth while.

In the Spanish burying-ground, steeped in
the white glare, one only finds a deeper and
more lasting sleep; and for the dreams, — the
flood and silence of light will suffice.

In this neglected spot, even memory seems
dead. The gate, opening on the dusty road, is
fastened by a twist of rusted wire, which leaves
a dull red mark upon the lichen of the crumbling post. The wooden crosses above the
sleepers are flaked and gray in the blaze of
sunshine; some of the cross-pieces have fallen,
and the white "I. H. S." has faded into the
weather-stained wood. A dried and withered
bunch of flowers placed very long ago on the

6

wiry brown grass at the foot of such a cross
shows Love's compromise with Death. " Mine
yet!" Love cries, and will not hear the answer,
" Mine; and thou art mine."

There is an old tomb here, covered with a
square coquina slab, which marks the grave of
" Catalina." It is well that the inscription was
cut deeply into the crowding shells, for the grave
lies under the shadow of a yew heavy with hanging moss, and in a little enclosure of broken
palings, which so shuts out the sun that the
lichen has grown thick across her name. The
side slabs are broken; some flowers stand
straight and sweet beside them; so tall that the
bell-like clusters rest as gracious hands upon
the top of the tomb; and all about through the
thin dry grass there is a little creeping plant
with a white star for a blossom. Perhaps they
were sown when "this marble covered the grave
of Catalina," and have grown from summer to
summer into joyous forgetfulness of the grief
that planted them, and the " *surpassing worth*"
that called it forth, — worth which was to make
it f eternal. " *She was called thus early into*

the silent land, leaving in the heart" — the lichen is very thick here — *"a record of sur-passing worth, which neither time can efface nor the changes of life obscure."* How this assertion, this throwing the gauntlet into the face of Time, betrays its own hopelessness! One hears, again, her stately name, as though sweet between the lips in one last cry for her, which has echoed even into the silent land, — Catalina! *" Set me as a seal upon thine heart, as a seal upon thine arm ; for Love is as strong as Death."* As strong as Death! Alas, Catalina, canst thou see this forgotten tomb?

There is a path from the broken gate, running straight between the graves, to a small chapel at the other end of the enclosure, where Mass has been said for the departed. Doubtless *"Antonia Jose Terriande de Muir, a native of Cadiz,"* who was *"lamented by a respectable circle of friends,"* was borne up this green pathway for that last moment of earthly pomp and honor, the brief rest before the altar steps ; then, out again into the blaze of sunshine, and the breathless hush of stifled tears and human wonder.

The rim of laughing sea mocks with its unchanged expanse the promises on the coquina
slabs of endless memory and regret, and con-
duces to trite reflections upon the vanity of

Life. In this forsaken burying-ground, overrun
by hens and dogs, and full of blossoming weeds,
with broken and neglected tombs, the readiest
thought, and for the moment altogether sincere,

is that Love, with its hopes and promises, is only a tiresome bit of cruel humor, and that Life is nothing better. "It is not worth while!" forgetting what was to make it so, forgetting the wind which blows the worlds into order and orbit.

These headstones mean nothing more than the beginning and ending of Vanity, one thinks, with the indifference of a dream. "Most of them recorded," says Addison of the inscriptions in Westminster Abbey, — "most of them recorded of the buried person that he was born upon one day and died upon another; the whole history of his life being comprehended in those two circumstances." And for the moment, so it seems.

One needs to leave this flooding stillness of noon, and brush the haze of golden light aside, to see again all the dear and daily things which lie between these two dates, "common to all mankind." If some fresh wind would but come up out of the violet silence of the sea, and touch his drowsy eyes and listless hands, a man might awake to see, serene and calm as a

great mountain which lies **unchanged behind**
its clouds, the familiar face of Life, **still smiling**
beneath the veil of dreams, and with her all
the happy train of simple duties which she
leads.

NIGHT.

" The heavens between their fairy fleeces pale
Sowed all their mystic gulfs with fleeting stars."

THE yellow light lingers upon the fort even
after the sun has dropped suddenly into
the sea; but a shadow creeps across the water,
and touches the sea-weed that fringes the base
of the wall, and then up and on, across the moat

and the portcullis. The coat-of-arms over the doorway, and the worn pulleys of the drawbridge on either side, fade into the warm dusk; all the barbican is wrapped in shadows: yet still the parapets and the towers for the sentry, hanging airily upon the four angles of the fort, are faintly flushed with rose, and the broad coping is warm beneath the hand.

It is not so easy to dream here. There is a detail in contemplation which robs it of its opiate, — a detail which never comes to him who, in the flood of sunshine, leans against a garden-wall, his eyes fixed on a glittering edge of shell. In the fort, too much is suggested; one cannot remember and dream at the same time. Besides, crumpling the water until it has the sheen of a web of silk, or stroking it smooth as with an invisible wing, which leaves a faint glisten in its gray track, the fresh wind blows the haze of sleep away.

The western sky throbs with an impalpable dust of gold when the sun has set: and the blue and cloudless day closes like the lid of a casket of jewels upon the violet rim of sea, and

shuts out the light. The crystal dusk grows cool
and fresh before the stars come out. Everything wakes; and the same alert distinctness
that touched the trees and bushes on Anastasia
Island at dawn, cuts the shadows out of the
twilight. Even the letters on the tablet beneath
the coat-of-arms over the entrance can be read,
although the years have blurred them until, in
some lights, they can scarcely be distinguished:
" REYNANDO EN ESPANA EL SEN^N DON FER-
NANDO SEXTO Y SIENDO GOV^R Y CAP^N DE ES^A
C^D SA^N AUG^N DE LA FLORIDA Y SUS PROV^A EL
MARISCAL DE CAMPO D^N ALONZO FERN^{DO} HE-
RADA ASI CONCLUIO ESTE CASTILLO EL AN OD
1756. DRI^CENDO LAS OBRAS EL CAP. INGN^{RO}
DN PEDRO DE BROZAS Y GARAY." One falls
to thinking of the sentry who used to stand
upon the wall, just over the coat-of-arms; what
dreams and hopes have shaped themselves here,
above this assertion, — for it is only that now, —
that the fashion of this world passeth away! A
little oval depression in the block of cement
shows how long the end of a spear or the staff
of a banner has rested there; through hours of

sunshine, and dim starlit nights, and in the fury
of great storms.   Always, there above the entrance, one sentry or another, living his own life
and thought, fancying both eternal, looking out
over the sea, and across the orange-groves to
the distant river, — loving, hoping, fearing; and

now, the sum of it all, a little depression in a
crumbling slab.

There is no watch now; the fort has nothing to fear.   Visitors come and go, or down
in the grass-grown moat a thin white donkey
wanders about, cropping hungrily at the tufted
thistles that stand in the angles of the barbican, or crowd like sentinels around a stone

which may have tumbled from the ramparts.
The offensive attitude of these thistles, brave
in green and silver, and with pink cockades,
is the only warlike thing about the peaceful
fort, — unless, indeed, one should except the
ants; they use a crevice, or a widening seam
between the great shell-stone blocks, for a
fortress and arsenal and store-house. How
very wide awake they are, these little bus-
tling red and black soldiers, tugging and pull-
ing at a burly dead bumble-bee, which one
of their scouts has found lying in his bronze-
gold armor under a clover-blossom! There is
a spider who would dispute their right to for-
age so near his preserves; but the ants per-
sist. They bring the dead general (he is
surely that, with his gold epaulets and the big
pollen-laden top-boots) up to the crevice in
the wall, and in a moment they are safe from
their gray poison-swollen enemy. Doubtless
they think the fort was built for them, these
brave little soldiers. It answers their needs
so perfectly that such a thought would not be
unnatural.

There are men who think that the great earth,
which went spinning through space when all
the morning stars sang together, was made for
them!

In the fading light, given up to thistles, and
with the whir of swallows' wings through the
dusk, the fort is so quiet it is hard to realize that it was ever the scene of stormy human life; that there were men here once who
watched this darkening expanse of blue with
keen and anxious eyes. They must have crept
behind the worn ramparts, to the round sentry-
boxes which hang like cages over the walls, to
look out from the loop-holes in hope or fear,
as might be the fortunes of war. And there
were those who suffered agonies of apprehension in the dungeons hollowed out of the rocks
below, while within sound of their misery other
men plotted and planned, with high ambition
or magnificent pride. For there is something
magnificent in transcendent folly; and such it
seems, now that they are all dead and gone and
there remains only a rusted ring in the wall, or
a half-obliterated coat-of-arms over the port-

cullis, to show that they
ever so much as
existed.

" Oh, but the long,
     long while the
     world shall last,
  Which of our com-
     ing and depart-
     ure heeds
  As the sev'n seas
     should heed a pebble
     cast ! "

But with the pebble's flying
instant, every law is as per-
fectly fulfilled as with the planet roaring
through empty and endless space; and so it
is, that pebbles are never done feeling their importance, refusing to remember that with the
splash at the end they are forgotten, no matter
what sparks their swift passage strikes out of
the indifferent air.

Here, in the fort, where much tumultuous
living has been swept into the past, the blank
of silence is stifling, and a curious fatalism would

persuade a man to yield himself up to those
laws which bear men and worlds into eternity
as a torrent carries straws upon its breast, and
in so doing find much that is beautiful and gracious, and nothing that is hard in his instant's
voyage. All this is in the air. It is inexpli-
cable, and leaves one with the query whether
Religions are not altogether a matter of climate,
— the wonder how many years it would take to
change a Norseman into Buddha himself.

The Sergeant, parrot-like and half asleep, has
many stories of this little greatness, or of that,
to tell of the fort. Very likely the stories have
grown with the years; but one does not look at
them too closely, — they belong to this luminous
dusk that blurs all the angles and arches of the
fort, and makes the line of sky and sea only an
advancing mist. The man's thread of memory
is strung with legends which go very far back.
He begins with Ponce de Leon, — a caballero,
already old, who has come to find the fountain
of perpetual youth. Already old, yet incapable of accepting age. What! had he not been

the friend and comrade of Christopher Colum-
bus? Did he not even now feel the passion of
success, which stirs the soul as wine stirs the
blood? Was not the spur of wonder still in his

side? He could not be old. His body might
be feeble, truly; but that was merely an acci-
dent of the flesh, a small matter. He was
young. His soul was as strong and glad and
brave as it had been fifty years ago. Old? No,
no, not he! All that he wanted was strong

7

muscles and clear eyes, — to cease to be ham-
pered by this miserable body which had played
him false at the very height of life.   So he
would go to search for that immortal water of
which every one had heard, but which, with all
the folly of a boy, he had scorned fifty years
ago.

One pictures to himself, here on the ramparts,
overlooking the level white beach, the pomp
and glory of that morning of Palm Sunday,
when Ponce de Leon set foot upon these Florida
shores.   The glitter of arms, the blaze of gold
and scarlet, the cross flashing in the sunshine,
and the solemn hymn which declared that there
was yet a Better Country, even an heavenly,
which the soul desired and with which it would
be satisfied, — so satisfied that it could forget
Youth and Life itself for entrance through its
gates of Death.

Yet there may have been a breath of relief
when the hymn was over, and the search might
begin for the fountain of earthly immortality.
Ponce de Leon's faded eyes may easily have left
the cross, and glanced towards the distant trees,

anxious to catch at once, under their blossoming
shadows, the flash and ripple of the wonderful
water. The flood of ineffable light, the lap and
murmur of the wrinkled sea, were all the promise
that his desire should be satisfied. There must
have been a moment of passionate and joyous
indifference to the hidden laughter of his soldiers, whose possession of what he sought made
them careless of his pathetic longing. Then
came the bitterness of hope deferred. Eight
weeks of search beneath the palms, of stooping
to drink with trembling hand at every spring,
of breathless waiting for that leap of the blood
which was to stir the shrunken veins across his
temples and light the old fire in his eyes; then,
with disappointment tugging at his heart, to set
sail again, — steadying his lips with promises
that he should yet find that for which Heaven
was an alternative.

After Ponce de Leon, came Diego Muruelo,
and then Fernandez de Cordova, who suffered
many things from the hands of savage men —
we are told; and, a little later, De Ayllon; one
by one, the last — the Sergeant has heard that

he was a very learned man — luring on board
his ships, from along this flowering coast towards the north, one hundred and thirty na-
tives; and then turning about for home. They
were to be sold; and that meant gold with
greater ease than by search in these hot sands.
But to a man they were set free in mid ocean,
for they died of despair and terror. A specu-
lator can only meet such a turn of fortune by
good-tempered impatience and greater wisdom
for the next time; so, carelessly, as a player
tosses aside a useless card, they were all flung
overboard, without a sail-cloth or a prayer,
and De Ayllon hunted for gold in less uncertain ways.

It was after this piece of treachery, that one
Pamphilo de Narvaez, to whom the King had
granted vast estates in this new land, came, full
of zeal for his own gain and the salvation of
souls. It was on the shores of the Bay of the
Holy Spirit, that he issued to the Indians that
extraordinary manifesto in Spanish which was
to insure temporal and spiritual benefit — to be
divided as the conqueror saw fit. This paper

was prepared for all the inhabitants of the lands
lying "between the River of Palms and Cape
Florida " — and he summons them to Salvation
in no uncertain words. " I, Pamphilo de Narvaez," he begins — " declare to you how God
created the world" — and he goes on to say,
that, although they will not be compelled to
accept Christianity, yet when they shall have
been informed of the truth they shall be made
Christians. " If you refuse," he says, frankly,
" with God's assistance, I will march against
you, arms in hand. I will make war upon you
by every possible means. I will obtain possession of your wives and children; I will re-
duce you to slavery." He further adds, that
all these threatened miseries will not be caused
"by His Majesty, nor myself, nor the gentlemen
who accompany me, but by yourselves only ! "

There is yet another story to be told, of that
sailor who climbed a tree in Panama, and saw
both oceans, and prayed that he might sail a
ship in the Pacific. He came here to the old
town, the Sergeant declares, and left death and
despair behind him, in place of the spoil he

took away. The Sergeant is not quite sure
whether this attack was before or after this
same sailor had crawled out upon the cliffs of
Terra del Fuego, feeling his way with strong
brown hands when the fog hung so thick across
great precipices that he could not see where he
was, and then, at the very last cliff, lying flat on
his belly, his chin out into infinite space, star-
ing with great eyes over the edge of the world.
He was a brave man, that Drake, the Sergeant
admits, but he had not much sense; what was
the use of risking his life in such a fashion?

But it was a very long time before this —
the Sergeant goes backward in his story — that
Ponce de Leon made his second landing, coming again, to search in desperate hope where he
had searched before. Memory of the gracious
sky, of the trees and flowers, of the hush of
dreams, tempted him to come once more; or
perhaps he felt vaguely that he had been young
eleven years ago, and so the Fountain of Youth
had not revealed itself to him, but now — now
that he was very, very old, so old that even the
longing for youth was dulled — why might he

not hope to find it? Perhaps, if he had waited, — if he had been content to sit in the sun, watching with drowsy eyes the ring of sea and sky, and forgotten to wonder or desire, — he might have found all things! He might have sunk into that unspeakable content with life, which does not know. Instead, he went away again, and died "in great bitterness." The Sergeant knows all about it. The Sergeant, dozing in the shadowy sweep of the great irregular arch, or walking in a pleasant dream back and forth across the blazing white courtyard, with never a fear or wonder or desire in his soul, knows quite well that old Ponce de Leon was a fool. But what of that? It is a good story to tell, and it is not the Sergeant's business to point out its folly: for that matter, all things are foolish when one comes to look into them, — all things that people make a fuss about, at least. Wisdom is calm; the Sergeant is very wise. He is not disturbed by any story he may have to tell.

There were men left to starve in that dungeon beyond, he says, passively; and against this wall, fretted with round holes, prisoners

used to stand to be shot. The grass grows thick
now on this side of the enclosure, because, he

declares, so
much blood has
been spilled on
the thirsty
ground.

There is the
dim outline of a
cross upon the
whitewashed
wall of a room
which was once
the chapel;
the Sergeant
has pointed it
out so often that
he himself scarce-
ly sees it now. Per-
haps because it is of no
especial importance in his vague eyes. The
bullet-holes outside, which meant the snap of
some short and brittle thread of life, interest
him as much as does this shadow of human

necessity, as eternal as the world, — this bridge between God and man. Or perhaps it would be more exact to say, interest him as little — for the difference between them is not great enough for choice. He thinks of them both with that contented indifference to all things which is in the air. The hint upon the chapel wall of the enigma of the universe is not more profound or more enticing than the mystery of the old coins which he threads between his fingers by the light of the flaring lamp upon the wall. He holds them close to his faded eyes to catch a glint of gilt through the tarnish of a hundred years, and wonders faintly from whence they came. His dim, gaunt face is in the gloom of the deep window, and his tall figure is only a clearer shadow in the dusk of the room.

" This one," he says, — " this one was in the hand of the skeleton we found below there in the dungeon; that one was washed about with the shells and pebbles on the beach; some ship went down, maybe, long ago, and this is the only sign of it above water to-day." He rubs

the coin gently between his tremulous fingers.
" This one was found in a crevice in the courtyard. Perhaps some Spanish soldier dropped
it, — it 's a Spanish coin, — see? A lady found
it. A lady in a gay frock, with a great white
umbrella, walking up and down in the sunshine.

It seems strange to see the ladies in their pretty
dresses here, and then think about other days.
Well, a lady does n't know a soldier's life.
There was a time when that court was full of
soldiers, and there was the roar of cannon from
the ramparts, — those very cannon lying buried
in the grass in the barbican, and green with
mould now, — and there were the scream of

bullets and the groans of dying men, and smoke
so thick you could n't see the flags!"

The Sergeant liked to think of it all sometimes,
and the rattling gallop of the drums, and the
fierce Spanish faces. But not often. It is better
to sleep in the sunshine, or watch the pomp of
sea and sky at the sunset gun.

It is curious how little distinct admiration,
how little keen individual delight, is felt in
watching these gorgeous skies when the sun
sets; or, later, in listening to the silver mys-

tery of the sea and stars. The soul slips into
it all in some strange way, and knows itself
only a heart-beat in the million heart-beats of
the pulse of God. The stately rhythm of the
waves folding along the shore is so certain in its
monotony that by and by the ear becomes unconscious of it; and there is the same uncon-
sciousness of the stars, swinging down like
censers through the darkness, each one a globe
of light, so soft, so joyous, that the whole eye
sees only light, and so is not aware of it.
There is nothing in the soul but a content
which knows no words and desires none.

Out in the rose-garden, in this soft glitter of
the night, the roses have lost their deep and
glowing colors, and have caught instead a pale,
phosphorescent light, as though each mirrored
dimly its own star. Shadows suck the greenness
from the leaves, and they are black, save for
glistening drops in the little notches along the
edge, while across the bosom of each flower the
dew is folded in a silver mist. The fragrance
of the roses is the dark air itself; it saturates
everything; it almost blurs the stars. It seems

strange that there should be the legend of passion and pain here, — lovers and gladness; the
tryst, and the heart-break afterwards; for there
is something as smothering to all emotion in this
overpowering sweetness as in the fumes of ether.
It is a relief to come back to the swinging water
beside the sea-wall, the clear black skies sown
with innumerable points of light, and the fresh
wind from across the palmettos on Anastasia
Island.

A sting of memory pierces through the down
of content, as the scent of the roses is blown
away; a thought of the keen brightness of
Northern skies; a hint of the clean and almost
bitter fragrance of yellow crocuses and pale,
cold snowdrops, — of that fresh, penetrating
sweetness of new grass, which shows its fright-
ened greenness under sodden leaves, along the
sheltered borders of meadows, or beside the
small springs of marshy orchards; of that subtle, faint, undetainable scent of the first white
violets, — of all the brave, glad life that greets
the north wind.

Oh, violet,
    'T is April yet,
The wind is cold, sweet maid ;
    For it doth blow
O'er lingering drifts of snow,
The ermine borders of Spring's velvet green ;
    Oh, art thou not afraid
    Thus early to be seen ?

THE COUNTRY.

8

THE COUNTRY.

THE RIVER.

"A league of grass, washed by a slow, broad stream
That, stirred with languid pulses of the oar,
Waves all its lazy lilies, and creeps on."

THE yellow current of the St. John's River
lies against the sky in a great curve towards the north; the farther shore is so low
and flat and dim, in the flooding light, that it

seems but a bank of mist, faintly golden in the sunshine.

The sweep of the current is slow and grave, so that, apparently, there is a curious fixity and permanence about it; it is without the hurry and noise of the little running rivers of the north, and it has none of their light-hearted intimacy, which comes from the crowding nearness of their trees and meadows. Not that the great river is cruel, — it is merely great; it has even an indifferent kindliness, — like the ocean or the sky, or a force in Nature. It bears a canoe as lightly and gently on its broad, smooth bosom as the most tranquil little pool might do, lying like a jewel at the feet of guarding hills; but if by some bit of carelessness, or confidence, a man trusts his life to it, it drowns him with smiling ease, and without the slightest effort to save him. There is no ripple made by an outstretched branch of tree or bush dipping into its waves like a friendly hand put out to rescue him; nor is there any knee of rock here and there above the water to which he might cling. It is very mighty and very beautiful; but it is not loved as a brawling northern torrent is, which tumbles anxiously about among its bowlders, or turns a mill-wheel in a green meadow; one does not trust it as he trusts the narrow rivers, freckled with sunshine in shallows under their leaning alders, where bare-legged children wade about, or fish with crooked pins, and empty spools for floats. True, even in these friendly and familiar streams, Death has pulled a man under the brown water once in a while; but that was surely because, in the first place, he was careless, and afterwards did not heed the invitation of their pleasant shores, and was not quick enough to catch at the branches thrust out for his aid from kindly trees.

Under a live-oak tree on the shore one puts his cheek down against the warm earth, and looks across the sweep of yellow water; on and on the eye travels, until the great waste of multitudinous ripples is lost in the sky beyond; the river pervades all space, it is supreme.

It is easy to realize how a river commends itself to the necessity of the soul for worship.

It calls forth adoration, as all things at once great and indifferent demand adoration. Very likely this passion for a great river, which stirs almost every man, springs from some twist in the brain left by an Aryan ancestor who prayed upon the banks of his holy river, offering his wreaths of lotus and his first-fruits of corn and wine to its majestic tide. There are many live-oak trees along these shores, under which the worshipper may build an altar and propitiate the river god; indeed, the trees are great altars themselves, hung with solemn moss, and murmurous with wonderful chords of that wind-symphony to which all Nature is a rhythmic accompaniment. To lie in the shadow of such a tree and look across the yellow water, which is barred by streamers of gray moss, is to worship without words.

These live-oaks are full of companionable whispers, and they have a very comfortable and friendly look; their gnarled and twisted limbs cover a wide space, and droop almost to the ground, shutting out the glare of light with misty curtains. One could spend a day with

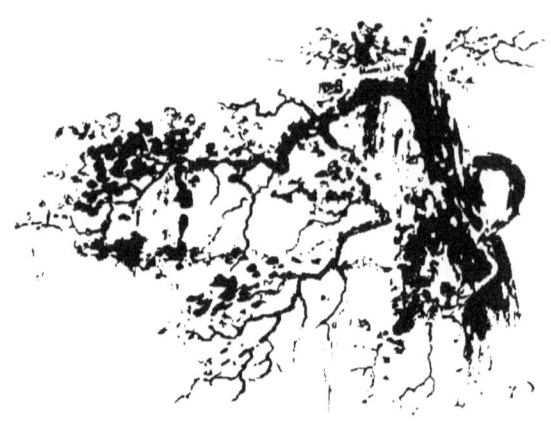

such a tree, and know no awe, but much rever-
ence. They are like certain motherly and un-
intelligent women, to whom one goes in grief
or despair, sure of being comforted and not too
deeply understood.

It is no wonder that that handful of French-
men whom Jean Ribaut left behind him at the
mouth of one of these southern rivers, as silent
and slow-flowing as the St. John's, with just
such gracious trees along its shores, should
have been "well content to have been forgot-

ten." Ribaut had brought them here, but had
only waited long enough to see that a fort was
built, and then he had returned to France, full
of promises of what he would do for them at
court, — how he would "imprint their names
in the King's ears," so that their "renown
should thereafter thrive unquenchably through
the realms of France," — as brave men, willing
to trust themselves to solitude and their enemies
for the sake of planting a colony in the King's
name. That said, he sailed away to find
" much weariness and care," which, naturally
enough, blotted promises out of his mind.

But for the twenty-six sailors left in their little
fort, everything was calm and peaceful; they
had no enemies to conquer, which might have
kindled their ambition, and, gradually, hope of
their commander's return became too blurred
to make them alert and keen. Their lives were
only sunshine and sleep; the fort upon the little
island they had chosen was overgrown with
grass; weeds sprung up about the cannon on
the crumbling ramparts. Time touched the
men so softly for a while, that one fancies they

would have been sleeping in the sunshine yet,
but for the fact of their ammunition running
low, so that their provisions failed, and perforce,
they woke to scan the horizon with anxious
eyes for Jean Ribaut's promised sail. But far
greater things had thrust their existence from
his thoughts; intrigue and civil war were more
important than the lives of a few men, dreaming under cloud shadows that chased across
the smooth waste of a great river or a land-
locked bay. So he did not return.

One falls to thinking of the final wrench with
which the garrison must have roused themselves
from sleep and starvation, and of that strange
ship in which a little later they floated out to sea.

" They built," some one says, "a small pin-
nace, though they had not a single ship-carpen-
ter among them. The cordage was of palmetto,
the sails their shirts and linen, and the vessel
was caulked with moss." The river bore the
strange craft kindly; perhaps the vessel seemed
to it — with rough logs, and twisted palms, and
flowing gray moss — like a part of the landscape,
some strange island which had floated from its

moorings, and had given shelter by chance to
these curious little creatures upon it; so the vast
current bore it safely to the ocean.

They must have grown less vague, these forgotten sailors, as the salt wind touched their
dreaming eyes, for they made every effort to
control this extraordinary ship, and strangely
enough, after unspeakable suffering and danger,
they did indeed go nearly half-way home; then,
"else they had all died," an English vessel found
them, and bore them back to France.

But the stupefaction of these deserted men, it
can hardly be called content, had fallen upon
them on their island under the live-oaks — one
cannot imagine that it would have happened,
had their fort been among the pines in the
barrens. There, of necessity, they would have
lived more eagerly, if less happily.

There is a keen insistence and perception of
life about the pines which is aggressive and
almost alarming. If nothing else, they confess
a man to himself too plainly. They flood him
with the glare of daylight, and their sparse,
severe branches are too far off for pity or inti-

macy. They do not dwarf him into a satisfied dream, as the live-oaks by the river do—they only press his miserable personality in upon him.

These lofty, slender trees, in endless procession, are full of individuality; they are like a straggling regiment where every man counts,

and the whole so spread out that it looks like
an army. There is very little grass about their
roots, and there seem to be no shadows upon
the deep, hot sand in which they grow. At
the top of each bare perpendicular shaft, the
horizontal branches spread like the radii of a
circle, making a cone which terminates in a
naked spike. "Their forests are silent as solitudes," Taine says. "The whistle of the wind
makes no noise; it glides over the stiff beard of
the leaves without stirring or rubbing them together. One hears no sound save the whispering
of the tops and the shrivelling of the little yellow-
ish lamels which fall in showers. The turf is
dead, the soil naked; you walk among pale shafts
which rise like tapers. A strong odor fills the
air, resembling the perfume of aromatics. They
live in families," he adds, "and expel other trees
from their domain." The impulse of worship is
not stirred among the pines; instead, there is
often a curious impatience with the assertive-
ness of the trees, and a dull fright at their
endless numbers.

It is strange that such multitudes of trees are

never thought of in a mass. It is always the
individual which presents itself to the mind.
Some one says of them, that they are count-
able, if one had but eternity; it is, he declares,
as if the observer " saw infinity," and he adds
that a " noise goes about through the high pine
needles which seems to formulate itself into that
lovely Latin song : —

> ' Infinitas ! Infinitas !
> Hic mundus est infinitas !
> Infinitas et totus est,
> Nam mente nunquam absolveris :
> Infinitas et illius
> Pars quælibet, partisque pars.' "

To wander for a day under their scanty shade,
among their endless files, the feet sinking deep
into the sand, and the eyes weary with their
lines and angles, is to be filled with a self-consciousness which produces the same irritation
mentally, which dust in the eyes does physically.
Their apparently endless stretch is unrelieved by
any hillside or rolling prairie, and is broken only
by the spongy inroad of a swamp, laced with
narrow creeks which widen into rivers.

The solitude is overpowering; the still air brings the strong balsamic fragrance in burning gusts, but there is no wind; at noon, on the barrens, even the dance of gorgeous butterflies and the clumsy booming of bumble-bees, cease; the stillness is appalling, and is never restful. It

is a relief to see any motion anywhere, — lizards slipping over a wrinkled root that buries itself in the sand like a veined and withered finger, or two buzzards sweeping upon rigid wings through the shadowless blue, in vast curves and circles.

It is a relief here in the barrens when sud-

denly night falls like a curtain upon the world;
darkness shuts out these appalling distances,
and lifts the weight of consciousness from a
man's soul. To lie between the wrinkled roots
of a great tree in the soft sand, which is warm
still from the flood of the sun, and look through
the spread of the branches at the near and
kindly stars, is to fall again into content. Perhaps it is the absence of mystery which is so
soothing. The skies reveal themselves in the
darkness, as they may not in the glare of day,
and the starlight, like a golden vapor, blurs
the endless files of the trees, so that they vanish
like ghosts a stone's-throw away, and the bene-
diction of darkness rests eyes which all day long
have been wearied by lines and numbers.

There are clearings here and there in the
forest, where pines are being felled, and one
may lean against a shaft which shall soon be
rocking between the sky and sea, — the mast
of a vessel, that will hold all the spars and
cordage, as the spine gathers the nerves and
muscles of a living man. There is a propriety

in putting a great pine in such a position, it is
so strong and so indifferent.   There is a strange
and interesting thing about these trees which
no one has yet explained — and the pines are
silent. When their forests are cut down for tim-
ber, there springs up instead of the pines, clean-
cut and virile, a whole undergrowth of bushy
young oaks! No one knows whence the acorns
came from which they sprang; there is often
not an old oak within miles, and the expanse of
sand had been covered with unbroken phalanxes
of pines.

Sometimes in the barrens one comes across
a single log-house, standing beside trees which
give it neither sympathy nor shelter.   True, the
occupants support themselves by the turpentine
which the pines supply.   They cut with clean,
even gashes a deep oblong in the bark, being
careful not to girdle and kill their source of
income; but any kindly feeling for the trees is
not to be imagined.

The lives of these people who collect the
turpentine, are very lonely and very vacant, but
their faces do not show that peace with vacancy

which is in the eyes of the men and women who live beside the creeks and rivers. On the contrary, there is a vague and restless self-consciousness which gives them a keener look, and hints at some deeper interest in life. Just what that interest may be is not apparent; possibly it is religion. It certainly is religion among the colored people, whose cabins are found in groups by the side of some scarcely distinguishable road which wanders across the barrens from one clearing to another.

It is almost a pity to define the one absorbing excitement of the negro as religion, but there seems to be no other word; and after all, grotesque and fierce as it is, surely it contains the essential element of all religions, — the abnegation of self.

Buddha, desiring to sink into —

> "nameless quiet, nameless joy,
> Blessed Nirvâna, sinless, stirless rest,
> That change which changes never;"

the nun in the convent, her pale cheek pressed against the cross in an agony of supplication;

9

the man of science, reflecting with passionate wonder upon illimitable space, sinking the
"string of thought into the fathomless," weighing the star-dust from the hand of the Unknown,
— all, surely, have the same ecstasy, the same
losing of the soul in the Eternal.   The method
by which it is reached — this loss which is gain
— we call religion; and the method differs with
the individual.   But the result — the absorption
into some greater force, and the consequent loss
of personality — is surely the same in every
case.

The means by which this half-civilized man,
the negro in America, attains the end which, in
common with the seer and saint, he desires, is
gross and crude, but it is sure.   He deliberately
prepares for oblivion.   "Getting happy," he
calls it; "getting religion," "getting the spirit
of the Lord."   But one must perceive that
although they call themselves Christians, this
savage worship of theirs is only a grotesque
caricature of Christianity.   The words " God,"
" Jesus," " Holy Spirit," are but tricks of expression, or rather the English for deities or

devils of their own. They are used with wild
cries and groans that gradually produce that
excitement or stupor which is happiness. Not
infrequently a point is reached where these
catch-words are dropped entirely, and it is only
necessary to continue the low chanting moan,
and consciousness of self is caught and drowned
in a great blind force which cannot be understood, but which is not feared.

It is curious to find how soon the anticipation
of this condition of mind begins to show itself
in negro children. This is, of course, because
they observe the extraordinary expression of
religion in their elders. Emotion and expression are synonymous in the mind of the African, — and reserve in Religion, or Love, or
Grief can hardly be imagined for him, — so
the negro child takes his own conversion for
granted, and the manner of it also, yet he is
apt — for he is keener than his white brother
of the same age — to discriminate in a droll
way, sometimes, between religion and conduct.
This promise of perception in him is not usu-
ally fulfilled; for mental growth ordinarily

ceases in the negro as childhood is left behind,
whereas the white man can acquire knowledge
far down the line of his years. Indeed, the
highest cultivation might almost be measured
by the ability still to increase.

Here in the barrens, in the silence that stings
and burns instead of soothes, there is a little
graveyard, fenced by palings, dazzling white in
the sunshine, and on the gate a darky girl is
swinging to and fro, singing in low, soft gut-
turals. Her attitude is full of lazy happiness;
but her little body is as lithe and alert as one
of the lizards which is sunning itself on a tomb-
stone that stands out clean and sharp in the
glare of light. Julia's black head has the glitter
and shine of a lump of coal, but her rolling eyes
are soft in spite of their brightness.

"I comes yere," she explains, "'cause my little sister she's burried yere. Law! wa'n't she
pretty? Wish 't you could 'a' seen her hair —
butiful! I likes to look in yere once in a while
at these dead folks. I'se sorry for 'em. 'Pears
like dey must want to know what's goin' on.
Law! I wish 't I knew what dey was doin'.

Cos, dey 's happy, playin' on harps; but seems as if dey might like to know what 's goin' on yere. So I comes and tells 'em sometimes. Cos, I talks most 'bout 'ligion, — 'ligion belongs to dead folks; I s'pose it would n't be righteous to talk of nothin' else. I tells 'em who 's got 'ligion in church. Cos, it 's only de Wash-foot Baptists church dat I go to yit awhile. When I gits growed up, and gits to know everything, I 'se a goin' to de Mefodists — it 's more polite at de Mefodists. Yes, soon as I gits 'ligion, I 'se goin' dere. But first, I 'se goin' to learn everything. I 'se goin' up norf so as to git all de learnin' der is. What does I think 'ligion is? Well, it 's bein' pious, as you might say; least, dat 's how you know if you 've grace, — grace dat 's done come to stay, — ef you 's pious. But, law! when you 'se gittin' 'ligion, you ain't stoppin' to be pious, always. I seen 'em when dey gits it; mostly, dey kick up dere heels, and cuss, and swar, and git happy. Dat 's 'ligion. Cos, afterwards, dey 's pious. So dey says. But mos' generally, mos' often, dey don't show pious."

And so she swings back and forth on the
gate, wondering a little about the dead folks,
planning for the time she, too, shall "be happy,"
— saying she will certainly go up North and get
" learning,"— unconscious that in a very little
while, five years, perhaps, or six, this keen wonder and interest, this desire to "know," will
all melt into a calm content with mere bodily
pleasure, chief of which is bodily forgetfulness,
named Religion.

The negroes have their own churches, in
which, as Julia asserted, distinctions of polite-
ness or fashion are drawn, because they say
" de Lawd comes to us diffv'ntly from white
folks. We-all can't help a showin' we 's happy,
as white folks does." So for miles through
the barrens, and from up and down the river,
they gather for their strange worship.

Sometimes one meets, early on a hot Sunday
morning, a whole family, perhaps the grandpar-
ents, as well as the father and mother and children, wandering slowly through the deep sand
of a half-broken road towards their church.

Their voices are melodious and gentle, their pleasant black faces full of sleepy kindness, but almost untouched by what is called spirituality. They sit, with apparent discomfort, but with the utmost good-nature, in an unsteady wagon; its canvas cover is stained with years of dust, and flaps lazily, where it is not tied with twine or rope to the framework of the cart. The white mule, between the shafts, walks in profoundest leisure, and is thin beyond words. The women are decorated, because it is Sunday, by bits of scarlet ribbon upon their dust-colored clothing, or a yellow neckerchief, perhaps, or a blue feather. The old negress wears a snow-white turban, and great gold rings in her ears; she seems to sleep, but from under her drooping lids her black eyes show in a line of glittering light. Thus, winding in and out among the pines, they reach their church.

The Wash-foot Baptists worship in a single room which is made of rough planks put together so carelessly that one can look out between the boards, and see the blaze of day

or the calm night, with its soft glitter of stars
above the pines.   A box serves for a pulpit,
and two flaring lamps in brackets against the
wall throw a glimmering and smoky light across
the dark faces.   The worship begins by a low
crooning hymn, rising and falling like the sigh
of the wind in the tops of the pines : —

> " O Lawd, wish 't I was in heaven to-night,
>   Wish 't I was in heaven to-night,
>   Wish 't I was in heaven to-night,
>   To see thy lovely face ! "

This chant changes as some new voice ejacu-
lates a different form of words, —

> " O pore sinner, man, Jesus wants ye yere,"

or —

> " O sweet Jesus, save my soul from hell ; "

and so on and on, a strange excitement rising
slowly in every face; a low rhythmical stamp
of bare feet on the wooden floor makes itself
heard, like a far-off roll of thunder, to which
the swaying body and the wreathing arms are
an accompaniment; through all this, a wild inar-

ticulate cry rises and falls above the chant. It is strangely unhuman, and so far as Christianity is concerned, save only for that one word "Jesus," it might be a heathen rite in the heart of an African forest.

The preacher, who is the master of the ceremony, urges the mad minds into greater fury

and greater joy. His scream or moan of denunciation, hope, despair, ends always in a wail without words; it is strangely like the cry of an

animal, quite without meaning, but containing
a thrill of power in the one vibrating note at
which it is pitched. "An' Jesus," he says, " he
go walkin' up Calvary (O–o–o–o my Jesus!) an'
what you got on yo' shoulder, Jesus? I 's got
a cross on my shoulder, — O–o–o–o!" And a
hundred voices moan with him, " Pore Jesus! "
"An' a collud man named Simon Cyrene —
Simon Cyrene — he take de cross, and carry de
cross, Jesus' cross — " " O pore Jesus! " comes
the murmur again; the soft stamp of the bare
feet rises to a muffled roar at the sound of that
name, and from every side of the dusky room
come shrill moans, and cries of " My Jesus! "
" Captain Jesus! " " Doctor Jesus! " " Save me,
Jesus! " The preacher grows so intoxicated by
the excitement about him that he is evidently
unaware of what he does. He puts the open
Bible across his bent shoulders and bowed
head, to typify the bearing of the cross; his
streaming eyes look up from under its shadow
as he staggers to and fro upon the shaking plat-
form. There are cries of " I 'se happy! I 'se
happy! " wild eyes fix and roll upward; a

strange and horrible smile stiffens upon poor dull features, and in a trance the soul forgets. A woman in this ecstasy flings her arms into the air with terrible shrieks, and the preacher stops his chanting prayer long enough to say, " She's happy — our sister's happy. Dere 's souls hangin' over hell to-night, in dis yere very room, lookin' at her maybe, — I wish 't dey was as happy as she is ! "

Through such preparatory excitement such a preacher leads his people until the moment comes for the celebration of a peculiar rite which in this especial sect accompanies the Sacrament of the Lord's Supper, — the washing of each other's feet. " De command of our pore Jesus," the preacher explains; and he then washes the feet of his elders, and they in turn those of the congregation, now thrilling and vibrating with the contagion of what seems insanity; all the while there is singing and wailing and broken shouts of prayer and exhortation. A woman, with sobs, breaks into shocking words, which however contain the Christian idea, —

" What heavenly man, or lovely God,
    Comes marching downward from the skies.
  Arrayed in garments rolled in blood,
    With joy and pity in his eyes ?"

As the ordinance proceeds, verses appropriate
to the occasion are lined out from a grimy
and battered little leather-covered hymn-book,
for most of the congregation cannot read.

" And did my Lord and Master say,
    ' If I have washed your feet,
  Ye also ought to watch and pray,
    And wash each other's feet ' ? "

There is surely but a step between this mad
excitement and self-mutilation or some monstrous orgy.   One almost trembles lest the
one protection to decency given by the Sacred
Name, no matter how meaningless its use, the
final reserve of civilization, be broken down,
and the savage leap into the light.   Yet who
would deny that the end of it all is religion,
the swallowing up of the individual in something greater than himself?

The result of this excitement is not obvious
upon morals; indeed, the minister remarked

candidly, and with simple curiosity, that he had thought that "de sisters was n't so pious in dere lives after one of dese yere times, do' he could n't just say why it was; maybe dey was tired!" And judging from the exhausted appearance of both men and women after such a meeting, the reaction from spiritual intoxication into positive immorality is not remarkable; but it gives the observer a curious sensation of distinguishing between religion and morals.

> " There was no motion in the dumb, dead air,
>   Not any song of bird or sound of rill.
>   . . . Growths of jessamine turned
>   Their humid arms, festooning tree to tree ;
>   And at the root through lush green grasses burned
>   The red anemone."

AFTER wandering for a day on the pine barrens, the traveller comes back into golden calm when the river is reached once more. It is peace to lie under a live-oak and slip into a pleasant dream, watching all the while the yellow flood of the St. John's.

This great volume of water rolls so slowly that one does not realize how continually it is carving out and bearing away the yielding shore. It thrusts its inlets far back into the woods or swamps, so that, like the features of a living face, the river is constantly changing; the more so, because its grave, deliberate cur-

rent is always building bars of sand, to which
it carries seeds and roots, until after a while
they glow like emeralds upon its golden shield.
Then, too, the grasses and lilies grow far out
upon the smooth flood; they are anchored to
the bed of the river by stems which lean along

the flowing stream until their length is twice
its depth; they encroach continually in one direction or another, so that the outline of the
low shore changes and blurs almost from day to
day. Wide fields of grasses ripple beneath the
ripples of the stream, until, here and there, the
river's vast expanse looks like a flooded meadow.
The cows stand breast-deep in the yellow water,
eating this sweet river grass; they seem to belong to the haze of sunshine and the drowsy air,
they are so still, and stare into vacancy with
such gentle, sleepy eyes.

Following in, and in, one of the curves carved
by the gentle persistence of the river and
crowded with lily-leaves, one finds suddenly
that the river itself is very far away. There is
only a line of yellow to be seen against a pale
sky, for the inlet has narrowed into a twisting
creek. It, too, is crowded with lilies, — broad,
rustling leaves, green and shiny, and supported
by long, strong stalks which spring from the
mud below. They are so instinct with life,
these lotus-like, almost transparent stalks, so
virile, so bold and glad, that the hand which

seeks to break one hesitates with a sense of crime. The dark, shining leaves rustle with a silken insistence against the curving prow of the

canoe, as though they would protect the sacred depths of the forest from which the creek has come to join the river. "Bonnets," these leaves are called; and looking across them to the

10

shore, from a canoe which lies motionless in
mid-stream, they are strangely like a crowd of
sun-bonneted women, nodding and chattering,
and thrilling with low, soft laughter. When
each " bonnet " is decked with blossoms, the
creek seems carpeted with gold and green;
not a glint of the still, brown water below is
seen, and save for the continuous and murmuring rustle, it would look like an expanse of
blossoming meadow which invites the tired feet.

How dim and shadowy must be the aisles between these brave green stalks, that bear up the
wonderful groined and fretted roof of spreading leaves. The midribs are the arches, and
here and there, through some narrow crack
or fluted opening, a single thread of light is
woven into the green stillness, and strikes a
sudden star from the water. Yet, like more
than one cathedral, life is outside of it and
around it, rather than in it. Gnats dance above
the leafy roof until all the quivering air glitters
with their delicate wings. Flies, with wonderful
cuirasses of gold and green, in helmets with
plumes of purple fire, and wings of silver sheen

spiked with jet, buzz with sleepy importance, or walk aimlessly along the edge of a leaf, or climb with evident toil up a broad, stiff blade of rush, to swing back and forth in the sunshine on its slender tip.

But the dragon-flies are most wonderful of all. The soft, still air, the checkered shadows on the water, and the shining blue heavens glitter with their unceasing dance; it seems as though a handful of jewels had been flung up into the sunshine, and, caught in its warm embrace, would not return to the earth again. They dart and circle; they poise, motionless, upon wings as tremulous as the light itself; their flight is a streak of pulsating fire; the air flashes with the dust of the gems which powders the green bronze of their heads. The sunshine in the middle of the creek is alive with them, and they pierce the shadows along the edge with zigzags of light; sometimes they stop to rest upon a gray cypress knee, letting their marvellous wings rise and fall in a sparkling rhythm, as though to some unheard music from the green aisles below the arching lily-leaves.

A cypress knee is glorified sometimes by a cluster of these sky creatures resting upon it, so that it seems to be decked with a jewelled crown or girdled by living fire.

Cypress knees line the edge of the creek, row upon row, until their numbers vanish in the gray stillness of the woods. It is easy to see their meaning,—these dull, living things, with no smallest share in the beauty of flower and leaf all about them. They are the purveyors and guardians of the great, grave trees from the roots of which they spring; they catch every floating leaf, every stray twig, all the soft débris of the creek or swamp, until by slow accumulation it forms a strip of earth, rich and black, to feed the trees and bushes which lift their green crowns into the sunshine. Sometimes the knees are quite covered by the earth which they have gathered, so that they themselves crumble and rot, and add their own lives to the mass of death upon which the giants flourish.

The middle of the creek is dappled with flecks

of sunshine; but along the banks, under the shadows of the leaves, it is only an occasional sunbeam which falls like an arrow through the gloom, giving a silver mystery to the stillness and green dusk of the woods, and touching a gray knee with a line of powdery light; often pale violets grow close to its shaggy side; or sometimes a lily strikes her threadlike roots into its wet, warm heart, and rests her exquisite whiteness against its rough bark.

Cypress knees are like occasional human lives, — most useful and most necessary, but not beautiful even to the kindest eyes, still less to their own. Still, what would become of progress if the strong and joyous souls, nourished by sacrifice of others, should suddenly and with dismay realize the cost of their lives, and refuse such growth?

These unlovely gray stumps of the swamp are never done with usefulness. They go down to the sea in ships, but it is not for them to feel the rush of spray, nor the dash through the green curve of a beckoning wave; they

cannot, like the trees which they have fed, trace great arcs against the sky as the vessel rolls and the masts strain and creak. Instead, below, in the darkness, untouched by wave or sunshine, they help to create the ship.

Easter lilies star the shadows all along the shore, growing in timid groups of two and three. Their white chalices are so pure and frail, and have a delicacy so exquisite, they seem but shadow cups filled with light; their stems are almost transparent, and if one holds the slender green shaft before the eyes, the crystal beat of the sap is like a pure thought in a child's soul.

Perhaps this is association, but it is curious
what moral qualities attach themselves to certain flowers, apart from that. Conceit in an
aster is as aggressive as it is in a man under
twenty; the sweet pea is at heart a wanton;
the fragrant bosom of a gorgeous rose holds
always a possible cruelty; one distrusts the
selfishness of the morning-glory; and as for
the peony — but criticism on her boldness is
superficial, — no one can really doubt her good
heart.

> A sturdy maid,
> Plump hands upon her hips ;
>   White throat flung back,
> And laughing, scarlet lips :
>   Full bodice laced,
> And kerchief well tucked in ;
>   Smile for each lad,
> (A kiss, perhaps, no sin !)
>   Plain speech, or rough,
> No empty flattery,
>   But wholesome heart, —
> That is our peony !

Here and there the green light — which is
sunshine strained through a net of leaves —

strikes a gorgeous blossom, a flake of palpitating
fire, or a golden disk, which seems as much out
of place here in the gloom, among the lilies
and the sober violets, as a cavalier among the
Quakers.   It is necessity, perhaps, rather than
history, which declares some such flowers for-
eigners.   There is a proud consciousness about
them, a hint of the beautiful and wicked world; a
flavor of the court, in fact.   One scarcely needs
the tradition of De Soto and his seeds.   If it
had not been De Soto, it must have been some
one else.   Captain Romans, perhaps; although,
indeed, his mind was upon more practical seeds
than posies for the women's gardens, which were
to break away into the forest, or wander along
the roadside, dreaming in the dank, hot shadows
or rioting in the sun.   For among the "artificial
produce" which Romans suggests should be in-
troduced into this new land, one only finds such
names as ginger, rye, and tea.

   Captain Romans, by the way, is so good as
to warn his reader that "no elegance of ftyle
nor flowers of rhetoric must be expected from a
perfon who is confcious that he is not fufficiently

acquainted with the language to write in fuch a manner as will pleafe a critical reader;" yet in spite of his modesty, one is startled to find how much vigor patriotism grants his words when he comes to speak of tea, which he thinks might as well be planted in the Florida barrens, or by these shaded streams, as in that other land of flowers. "Tea" he describes as "a defpicable weed, and of late attempted to be made a dirty conduit to lead a ftream of oppreffion into thefe happy regions, . . . it would not have deferved my attention, had it not fo univerfally become a neceffary of life, and were not moft people fo infatuated as more and more to eftablifh this one article of luxury in America; our gold and filver for this dirty return being fent to Europe." He ends by calling it a "monopoly of the worft kind," and insisting that the realization of this ought to "roufe us to introduce the plant into thefe provinces, that we may trample under foot this yoke of oppreffion which begins to gall us very fore."

De Soto, however, when he planned to bring his seeds from Spain, had no resentment or am-

bition to express, there was nothing in his mind
but paternal care for his colonists. He meant
that the familiar faces of the dooryard blossoms should make this new land hold a look of
home. So, in that long march through the
wilderness, across the endless barrens, around
terrible swamps, or by the silent windings of
the creeks, the seeds were scattered with lavish
hands, — some for use, some for beauty, all for
that homelikeness which was to make life better for these transplanted souls.

The story would be fairer if Truth did not lay
her finger on the page that tells it, and bid the
reader spare De Soto his praises for bringing
old-world blossoms into the new world. The
fact was, that only the impulse was De Soto's,
the act was left to his followers. Before the
dawn of that Whit-Sunday which found his
fleet in the great Bay of the Holy Spirit,
before even he had set sail from Spain, he
had given his heart to the lovely Lady Isabella; so, naturally, it had been easy for the
_hing lover to forget fame and fortune, as
well as plans for the welfare of his colo-

nists. To be sure, having won her, the old adventurous spirit came back, and he was off again, — for one must pursue something, — only remembering her beauty and her charm long enough to sigh a little when the stars came out and the sea was smooth, and swear he would return again; meanwhile leaving such small things as seeds, or plans for the conversion of the barbarians, to his men.

He did not sigh so often, it is said, when he found, toward the North, that race of Indians whose queen was a woman, and beautiful. A man were surely ungracious to sigh when a lady loosens from her own brown throat a rope of pearls, each one gleaming like a star in a mist, and puts it about his neck. Beside, if the Lady Isabella shall one day wear the royal gift, why not, like a gallant gentleman, — if an absent husband, — bend a little lower and kiss the bronze cheek? For one must fancy that "the brave, the virtuous, the magnanimous Captain Don Fernando De Soto" swore within himself, as he looked into the languishing eyes of the dark Princess, that he would one day twist

these same great pearls around his lady's neck,
although, perhaps, with no words about this
scene under the live-oak trees by the river, or
the kiss, which, it appears, carries the same
meaning in the Floridas as upon the banks of
the Mediterranean.

That he returned the brown lady's " very gracious speeches of love and courtesy" no one
can doubt; for seeing himself repentant in advance, it was but natural to feel already forgiven,
and so "go joyously for many days."   Those
hours, however, which are to strike a balance,
and atone by works of supererogation for past
ins, do not always dawn. So many failures

came, so much disaster,—even the pearls were
burned!

De Soto still sighed, but his sighs were not like
those which had melted into the music of waves
and shining stars and soft winds, when the commander had looked back towards the land which
held his mistress. Now, three years in that terrible wilderness -- three years of alternate hope
and disappointment, of steady loss and of continual toil—had brought new thoughts into his
brave, high heart. Looking over that yellow
flood of the Great River,—for so they called the
Mississippi,—so far from that young wife upon
whom his mind dwelt with painful persistency, so
very far from what her thought of him may have
been, he died. "The next day being the 21st
of May, 1542, departed out of this life the valor-
ous, virtuous, and valiant Captaine Don Fernando
De Soto, Governour of Cuba and Adelantado of
Florida;" whom, says the chronicler, "fortune
advanced as it useth to do to others, that he
might have the higher fall. He departed in
such a place and at such a time, and in his
sickness he had but little comfort."

The creek is full of quiet life; a sensitive
person might be conscious that he was an intruder, from the glances of calm surprise, and

from annoyance, which are turned upon him as
his canoe startles this or that land or water
It would be well to go hat in hand past
ator, who may roll like a black log from
into the water, too disdainful of human

rudeness to allow himself to be looked upon.
Yet before he dives he will turn a cold, small
eye in the direction of the canoe, and a month
afterwards the memory of that stare will make
a man shudder and quite forget that the dull,
dark creature may have had any interests or
pleasures of his own in the proprietorship of
the creek.

Yet here and there an intruder does appreciate him; one traveller, coming upon him
silently in a little lily-crowded cove, declares
him to be a "very honest and worthy saurian
of good repute." And he falls to describing
the house of his saurian, with a nice sense of
his own smallness and his friend's greatness.
He is a very Boswell for details. "It is divided into apartments," he says, "little subsidi-
ary bays which are scolloped out by lily-pads
according to the sinuous fantasies of their
growth. My saurian, when he desires to sleep,
may lie down anywhere; he will find marvellous
mosses for his mattress beneath him; his sheets
will be white lily-petals; and the green disks of
lily-pads will straightway embroider themselves

together above him for a coverlet. While he
sleeps he is being bathed. What glory to awake
sweetened and refreshed by the sole careless act
of sleep!"

Turtles also watch the intruder; there is a
condescending curiosity in the way in which
they stretch up their long, thin necks to observe
him, but they easily lose countenance, and drop
bashfully down into the water when he returns
their stare. The snakes are the only really
timid and deprecating denizens of the creek
and swamp. Doubtless they have been made
to feel their outcast condition by their less ob-
jectionable neighbors, who have watched the
unfailing antipathy of men for these beautiful
and often harmless creatures. In this silent
progress of the canoe into the forest, one
comes upon a snake lying across a cypress
knee, lithe, black, shining, with alert, uplifted
head and diamond eyes, half in and half out of
the water, ready at the first splash of the paddle
to drop and dive, swimming across the creek
in wonderful gleaming curves. It is strange
how few can appreciate his beauty or feel his

charm. The intense aversion which serpents arouse in almost every one, must, of course, be traditional and inherited, as it is felt for the innocent and pretty garter-snake as deeply as for the Crotalus horridus of South America, which is most hideously ugly as well as venomous. This terror is as old as history, and more than one trader upon human credulity has used it to win power or gold or fame.

One thinks of that little sunshiny town of Abonotichus on the south shore of the Black Sea, and the beautiful youth Alexander, the Cagliostro of the second century, who had eyes like jewels, and a "sweet and limpid voice." How well he understood this fear, which has glided like a living serpent into all mythology! One can fancy his secret mirth at the instant subjugation of the simple villagers when he proved himself the prophet of Æsculapius by displaying about his neck and body the glittering coils of the enormous python, on whose head he had affixed a human mask. The force of this traditional terror is seen when it is recalled that even Lucian was for a moment deceived; the predisposition to be awed by a serpent was in the wise man, and in spite of his antagonism to the prophet he could not resist it. It would seem that intelligence, like holiness, is not always a protection against the freaks of the imagination; and it is most interesting to observe, in connection with the unreasonable fury which is felt by men for snakes, how greatly the serpent has affected the history of the race.

A man's desire to kill a snake never leaves him. Here, paddling noiselessly up the creek, so steeped in the wonder and beauty of the woods and water that he cannot even remember the bitterness and passion of yesterday, a man will suddenly and violently fling himself out of Nirvāna, because he has caught sight of a moccasin. To kill the pretty creature, sunning himself on a cypress knee, quite harmless, at least for the moment, because entirely out of the track of the traveller, he will leave Paradise. And he is aware, too, of a new, unwonted cruelty in his soul. That the snake slips into the water, his glossy back cut and broken, with

hours of agony before death comes, does not
distress him at all; his only regret is that his
paddle was split in the encounter, and the canoe
has to be pushed from a mud-bank on which
it has grounded. Of course, this blind rage
which kills the cold and gliding outcast of the
swamp has nothing to do with the passion of
the sportsman. In that, there is a generous
appreciation of the prey; it is the instinct which
bade Walton, in putting a frog upon his hook,
"use him as though he loved him," — with
all the gentleness of which the circumstances
admitted.

The water of the creek, which winds far back
into the woods, is very still, and so clear that it
makes the stream a mirror. The drift of dead
leaves lies black below the motionless current,
so that all the reflections are pictured in a sort
of luminous darkness, like a Claude Lorraine
glass; but they are marvellously distinct. Were
it not for the faint lap and gurgle against the
prow, and the slow splash of the paddle, one
might fancy that the canoe floated in mid-air,

the sky above and below, and that he had
begun a flight among the tree-tops.

A cypress at the water's edge rises in a su-
perb pillar, with a capital of circling branches
which seems to hold up
the low and dazzling sky;
but in some wonderful
way the whole mag-
nificent shaft is

repeated in the mirror of the creek; it apparently separates two heavens. At a little distance it is almost impossible to say where the
tall bank meets the water and the reflected

bark begins. The canoe rolls and dips as the gazer leans upon its side and looks down into the sky and branches; indeed a canoe so adapts itself to the motion of the occupant that it seems to be part of the man himself, — he feels vaguely, half fearfully, that he has no support, that he is floating in these repeated heavens, with infinite space below as well as above. A man who takes the paddle in his hands for the first time, here on the creek, achieves that very rare experience, — a new sensation. He understands the exhilaration of a bird's flight, or the buoyant rest of a fish in dim sea-depths; he knows the wonder of the soul without a body, born into the mystery and stillness of death.

This experience cannot come in a row-boat, which is too material, one might almost say too dogmatic; a row-boat, in fact, has all the self-consciousness of civilization, for only civilization could make a man content to turn his back in the direction of his progress with the assurance of safety. His canoe, on the contrary, — and it will be observed that it should be a birch

canoe, — effaces herself as completely as though
she had a soul. He could tell her the secret
of a hopeless love without any fear that she
would intrude her own personality, and with the
same certainty of being understood that he has
when he whispers his sorrow to his dog, or
broods upon it half aloud by the side of a running stream ; or, indeed, he could tell her any
of those primal distresses or perplexities which
bring the soul whimpering to the heart of Nature. And his canoe is forbearing as well as
sympathetic. This leaning far over to look
down into the reflections is really carelessness
of the laws of her being; but she endures all
such slights nobly. No doubt she understands
the wonderful beauty of the picture in the
stream, as well as the man does.

There are long banners of moss hanging from
the branches of the trees; and looking down
into the water, they seem to stir and wave with
the unseen ripple of the creek. Above, all is
perfectly still; the moss hangs like mist about
the cypresses. It is as though Night's cloak had
caught upon the bare, sharp twigs as she fled

before the golden trumpets of the dawn. These gray banners fall so straight and long that here and there they touch the water and float a little way with it; indeed, their slight inclination is

the only indication of the current. Sometimes, while the wind has yet its morning freshness, these streamers wave and swing a little in the sparkling air, and catch and tangle, and then blow free again; but generally they hang like

filmy bars of cloud against the still, deep blue
of the sky.

Looking into the woods from the canoe, the
tops of the trees are blurred and dim with

moss; it seems as though they were wrapped
in cobwebs; only their great trunks stand clear
and regular in the morning light, with the blossoming bushes and the dim procession of the
cypress knees about them.   Even when the
wind blows, these mossy trees are soundless;
one misses the silken rustle of the Northern
woods, hearing, instead, only a noiseless whis-

per and smothered murmur, as though feathers
blew against one another. The reflections of
these great folds of moss are so wonderfully
clear, that at times, instead of floating through
mirrored tree-tops and blue skies, the canoe
seems to drift across banks of gray, still clouds;
but that is when the moss has quite covered and
killed the trees upon which it hangs.

For the most part, it is the fresh and living
green which is mirrored in the crystal darkness
of the creek. There is such wonderful greenness in these forests which march beside the
creeks, that their leaves have a certain vigor
about them which is almost light. The lurk-
ing shadows under the great branches have
green tones in them; the very air itself is luminous as an emerald, shimmering with the pulses
of the sun which the matted boughs have shut
out. One looks down the aisles of the woods,
and sees green nets of shadows stretched from
tree to tree, quite motionless, and unstirred by
any wandering wind; only showing here and
there a gold thread of sunshine braided down
among them.

THE MEN.

"'T is life, whereof our nerves are scant,
O life, not death, for which we pant;
More life, and fuller, that I want."

FLOATING noiselessly through this inverted
heaven, this absolute stillness and grave
reserve of Nature, it seems part of it all to come
upon a Cracker, fishing from a dugout which
is anchored under a dead cypress. His motionless face shows an indifference to life — his own
or other men's — as profound as that of the
tree at his side. There is a woman with him
in the water-logged and decaying boat, and
both have a look of permanence about them, —
of having been here, beneath the moss of the
great tree, always. One cannot think of them
anywhere else; they are part of the landscape.

If the author of " Plain and Eafy Direc-
tions to Navigators, with account of the Two
Floridas and the Dangerous Gulph Paffage,"

could ever have seen these strange people,
who make their homes in the solitudes of the
swamps or forests, his assertion concerning the
original inhabitants of Florida would seem to
have been written for them instead of for the
Chickasaws and Tocopocas.

"I am firmly of opinion," he declares,
"that God created an original man and woman
in this part of the globe of different fpecies
from any in the other parts. Let the learned fay
all the fine things that wit, eloquence, and art
can infpire them with, of the fimplicity of pure
Nature, and its beauty and innocence. The
favage wretches of America are an inftance
that this innocence is a downright ftupidity,
and this pretended beauty a deformity, which
puts man, the lord of the creation, on an
equal foot (yea, below) the brute beafts of
the fields and forefts."

The Indians, of course, were in his mind as
he wrote; but looking at these expressionless
faces, one applies his words.

Perhaps that quality in an occasional friend
which makes it possible for us in imagination

to place him anywhere on earth or in heaven,
is his humanness. He is the same man, although our mind's eyes see him among Arctic
snows, or in the yellow glories of the court of
Pekin, or at the gate of Paradise. He is always perfectly congruous. He adjusts himself
to the " celestial everywhere," finding a path
to Infinity in everything finite. These silent
people of the swamps and woods, on the contrary, can only be thought of as upon the very
spot where one chances to find them; and as
this feeling of their permanence increases, the
less human they seem to be, — less human, not
at all in the sense of brutishness, but only that
they become more and more a part of physical
nature, less and less spiritual expressions of
God. They have not even the individuality of
the moment. It seems as though they were as
unchangeable and lasting as the woods and the
stream, and they have apparently no more personality. One reads nothing in the lines about
their vague lips or in their indifferent eyes; not
because there is any slightest veil of reserve, but
only because there is, it would appear, nothing

to conceal. Their blank impassive faces are to the eye of the passer-by exactly alike.

An observer cannot escape the feeling that the members of a Cracker family must have been touched by exactly the same sensations of apprehension, — which would hardly be called thoughts or emotions; and he admits that he would have to live among such people before he could discover their characteristics, just as he would have to live in the barrens before he could distinguish individual pines in the monotonous and endless armies of these trees; and it would seem as though he could scarcely receive any more sympathetic companionship from these silent men and women than from a group of pines full of murmuring whispers.

Crackers do not often care to live in settlements or villages; instead, each small household dwells in a cabin that stands quite apart; it is built generally on a little spot in the woods, which has been cleared by toil that was almost as slow and patient, and as without feeling or interest, as a force in Nature.

To come out of the silence of the forest into

this silence of souls is profoundly strange.
There is something almost awful in seeing
these motionless beings in their dugout under
the dead cypress. Their eyes are without spec-
ulation, their monotonous voices are pitched in
that key which the wind strikes sometimes in
the pines, and there is as little will or choice
in their tones as in its soulless diapason. They
have dim, sad faces, which have yet known no
sorrow; being sad only as the woods are sad,
because there is no capacity for grief.

The household of a Cracker family dispenses
often with necessities, — perhaps because they
are considered luxuries; while the comforts
which it enjoys might be summed up in one
word, tobacco. The roof of their cabin is apt
to be crumbled and broken; the shingles are
curled and warped under cushions of green
moss, and along the eaves, during the rainy season, they are almost hidden by the soft growth
of tree-ferns. It is, however, inconceivable that
a leaking roof should be mended while there is
yet a to-morrow in which such work may be

done. The walls are of logs, the spaces between them being plastered with mud; there
is often no window; instead, the door stands
open, letting a square of sunshine fall upon the
earthen floor; sometimes a dancing glimmer
from the creek upon whose bank the cabin
stands, strikes on the ceiling, and runs in rippling light across the logs. But that reflected
light from running water is, strangely enough,

not cheerful. Should it rain, and the door be
shut, — why, then, sleep. For why should one
spend the empty hours looking from a window
into the dank and streaming woods, when sleep
is possible? The floor is higher in the centre,
so that the rain dripping from the broken roof
may not stand in pools about the feet; and
for such weather the logs burning in the big
fireplace give some comfort. The wide hearth
is at one end of the single room, — which is the
whole house, save for the loft above, — and it
at least is cheerful, with joyous flames, and soft
snaps, and the laughter of the bubbling sap in
green logs. But the lustreless eyes do not
brighten with the dancing light, the fire is only
merry for itself.

The chimney is on the outside of the house,
and is built of mud, and girdled by barrel hoops
or ropes which were put around it to support
it while the mud was wet; but as the fires
within dry it, it is apt to lean away from the
wall of the house, as though with a sort of annoyance and disgust at the occupants. For the
most part, however, except in the rainy season,

the Crackers prefer to cook out of doors, and so, near the cabin, a fire is built between three great stones, which serve as a tripod for their kettles, and a thin twist of blue smoke as straight as a staff rises into the still air.

Here these human beings live, — if it can be called living. One wonders if there is any home feeling in their vacant minds. There is almost no conversation between the heads of such a household, and why should there be? The same vague dreariness infolds them both, the same absence of interest paralyzes them, the same indifference shuts out emotion.

In these cabins one is met by the anomaly of a face which belongs neither to youth nor age, and is at a loss to find an adjective which describes it. There is no experience stamped upon the forehead, so the man is not old; there is no hope in the listless eyes, therefore he is not young. He knows neither necessity nor desire; only silent, joyless, painless existence, which is as perfect in its way as a tree or a stone, and as entirely in place. It would seem that such a face has always been, and must

always be. Death has apparently forgotten it,
and life has never known it; it is without
intelligence, yet not the face of an idiot.

These people are shy, and somewhat suspi-
cious, but not unkind; there is often a strange
disinclination on their part to look directly at
their questioner. They glance downward and
sideways with the same anxious embarrassment
which comes into a dog's face when his master
looks searchingly into his eyes.

Very likely, if one of these Crackers could
arouse himself from the pleasant stupor of the
drowsy noon, he might pity the eager lives of
men who have once had hope, and now have
experience; who wonder and desire and suffer.
Of course such pity would be resented with
contemptuous amusement. But who shall say
that there is not equal arrogance in men who
pity the Crackers for a contented calm which
their own intense and earnest lives have never
known? Besides, our disgust is the protest of
what is possible in us; and we must certainly
admit, in spite of the horror we feel for a
human existence which is not life, that this

condition of things is almost inevitable What would happen to any fine, clear intellect after a score of years in this appalling solitude of the forests and swamps, this climatic exhaustion, with bad water and bad food, and, more than all, with no ambition? Having grown chiefly toward the ideal, would it not, before the great realities of Nature, shrivel to a level far below the savage, whose progression has been away from the ideal, and entirely in the direction of daily and practical needs? But instead of a score of years, there have been many generations to bring about this condition which shocks the traveller from the North. So that, although such degeneration in the once keen, glad Saxon is astounding, even the most casual passer-by must feel that it is circumstantial.

When the canoe, silently, with the wake of the steering paddle behind it, comes drifting down the creek in the late afternoon light, the man and woman in the dugout are still fishing under the shadows along the shore. Perhaps their boat has floated a little farther down the stream; but that movement of Nature seems to have been only one since the canoe passed them earlier in the day. The man, with clay-colored face and hair, and pale, unseeing eyes, still leans his stubbly chin upon his hand in precisely the same attitude which he had assumed four hours before; it does not seem as though he had stirred; he stares without meditation and without perception at the clear water. The woman holds her rod — a peeled branch of elder — at apparently the same inclination at which it was earlier in the day. Her faded and stained pink sunbonnet hides a face without any of the gentleness of womanhood; her gaunt wrists, her lean, frail body are without the grace of softened curves and color. She glances up for a moment, but there is no inquisitiveness in her sad eyes, and then she looks again into the water; there is not the faintest brightening of interest in her face, when her companion begins to answer dreamily some tentative questions; his replies, however, are only monosyllabic. Nor is this because she has a greater interest either in her own thoughts

or in her successful angling; for although she
draws in her line with a fish struggling and
flashing upon the hook, she never glances in
triumph or pleasure at her companion, as she
pulls it off slowly, drops it into the bottom of
the dugout, and baits again. Perhaps the man
does not see the creature flapping and gasping
at his feet, the light glittering upon scales as
wonderfully iridescent as bits of Roman glass;
at least, he never looks at it, or at her, or at
his interlocutor.

"Do you catch many fish here?"

"Some."

"What are they?"

"Sunfish."

"It is very still here in the woods; does n't
it often seem lonely?"

"Do' know." His voice is as vague and far
away as a voice heard in a dream.

"But it is pleasant to be alone sometimes,
is n't it? — one likes to think."

No reply. An impassive stare at the gunwale
of the canoe; one cannot imagine that the pale
eyes could be lifted higher.

"Do you think it is better to live in here quietly and pleasantly, or to be in a great city and have noise and thought all around you?"

The man shakes his head vaguely. There is a faint, helpless anxiety in his face, which is almost pathetic; he even sends a shifting glance toward his companion, — and is silent. He seems incapable of answering. One says good-by, perforce, and a turn in the creek hides the two motionless figures, leaving the observer with an odd feeling that they belong to the land-scape, and that they will be there in the crumbling dugout, under the moss of the dead cypress, a hundred years hence.

The difference between the Crackers who exist here now, and the Indians who once paddled noiselessly up and down these still rivers, is most striking. The solitude and appalling shades did, to be sure, give the savages a certain gravity, but they were not thus dead while they lived. In the Indian no soul had been stunted, because no soul had been evolved;

and the result was a simple joy of living, — not intense, perhaps, but also not vague. Indeed, looking into these vacant faces of the Crackers, it is a relief to remember that there ever was any animation, — anything eager and interested, here in the swamps or forest. The braves had their ambitions — whether the ambitions were lofty or not has nothing to do with it; they meant thought, and an expression of the wish to live. The women had curiosity, perhaps, and even vanity. In a word, they were human. In the pleasure of knowing that, one does not stop to inquire whether it is wise to be human or not.

It is delightful to read of the living instincts which were once here. Some old traveller — interested but disapproving — tells of the luxury visible in the dress of the Indian women, and mentions an instance of "female fondnefs of drefs" which seems to him especially surprising. " I obferved," he says, " that the women dreffed their legs in a kind of leather ftockings hung full of the hoofs of the roe deer in form of bells, in fo much as to make a found exactly like that of caftagnettes. I was very defirous of examining thefe ftockings, and had an opportunity of fatisfying my curiofity on thofe of my landlady at her return home. I counted on one of her ftockings four hundred and ninety of thefe claws. There were nine of the women at the dance with this kind of ornament: fo that, allowing each of them to have had the fame number of hoofs, and eight hoofs to a deer, there muft have been killed eleven

hundred and ten deer to furnifh this fmall
affembly of ladies. An inftance of luxury in
drefs," he adds (and one can see the uplifted,
deprecating hands, the frowning brows, the keen
eyes looking over the silver-bowed spectacles at
the decorated legs of the obliging landlady), —
" an inftance of luxury in drefs fcarcely to be
paralleled by our European ladies ! "

But following the narrow creek farther into
the woods, it is easier to understand the apathy
of the men and women who live now in these
endless shades. Nature is so triumphant, so
fiercely insolent, that it seems folly to oppose
the human mind to her.

As one loses sight of the man and the woman
in the dugout, leaving them in the shadows,
and winding on into the heart of the forest, he
finds the creek growing very narrow ; but the
clear water, checkered by spots of sunshine, is
still deep ; the branches of the trees begin to
meet, and form a green and arching roof, with
openings here and there like windows with
flowing tracery, through which come wavering
lines of light to dance upon the dark water ; the

gigantic cypresses, whose trunks widen suddenly towards the roots, tower up quite bare of
branches, except at the very top, and these are
draped with long folds of moss; the soft, fresh
green of the other trees is blurred too by the
insistent growth of the parasite, and with it a
tangle of vines — flowers, and tendrils, and
broad shiny leaves — hangs in a flowing curtain
over the creek; often the prow of the canoe
can scarcely push aside this embroidered arras
which shuts in the deepening mystery of the
woods; Easter lilies gleam in the heavy shadows like single stars, but their fine whiteness is
only the fringe upon Nature's massive vest-
ments, which, rank and heavy, press the life
out of the stagnant air.

This monstrous vegetation overpowers
thought; it crushes so light and slight a thing
as mind, as a man might crush the shell of a
humming-bird's egg between his thumb and
finger; it seems as though it would dominate
earth and heaven, marching with a sort of dumb
and ferocious joy, and trampling everything
which opposes it under its triumphant feet.

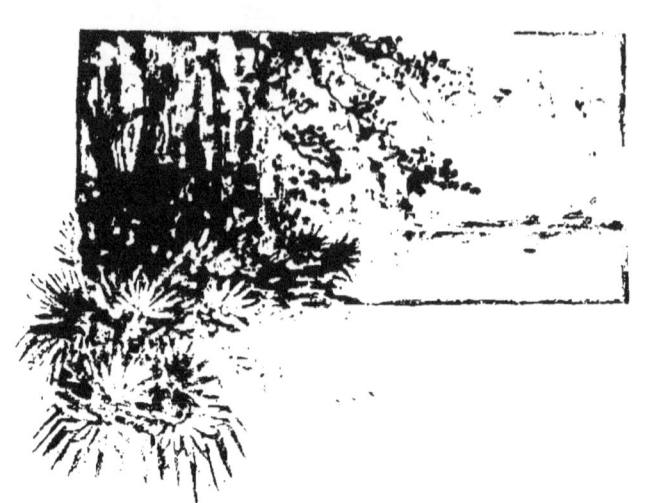

Such green dusk and intense silence, threaded
by the sparkling flight of a darting dragon-fly,
is a fit setting for that picture of man and Nature
which was drawn by a poet who felt the appalling
difference between the great and little. He
sees, he tells us, "the majestic form of a woman
clothed in a loose green dress. With her head
supported in her hand, she seems sunk in profound thought." He realizes that this woman
is Nature, and he says: "A reverential fear,
like a sudden shiver, penetrated my soul. I
approached her, and greeting her respect-
fully, I cried, 'O Mother of us all, on what
are you meditating? Are you perhaps thinking of the future fate of mankind, or of the
long road man must travel in order to reach
the greatest possible perfection, the highest
happiness ? '

"The woman slowly turned her dark, terrible
eyes, her lips moved, and with a thundering,
metallic voice she spoke : 'I am considering
how to give greater strength to the muscles in a
flea's leg. The equilibrium between attack and
defence has been lost, and must be restored.'

" ' What!' stammered I. ' Is that what you are thinking about? Are not we men, then, your dearest, favorite children?'

" The woman frowned slightly, and said: ' All creatures are my children. I care equally for you all, and annihilate all without distinction.'

" ' But virtue, reason, justice?' I stammered.

" ' Those are human words,' resounded the brazen voice. ' I recognize no good or bad. Reason is no law for me; and what is justice? I gave you life; I take it from you and give it to others. Worms or men, it is all the same to me.' "

The realization of his own insignificance which comes to a man here in the forest or swamp is not good. For the soul to be flung upon its face in the dust, permanently, can only result in the kind of living which the man and woman in the dugout experience. It is a relief to stop paddling and drift backwards down the stream until a spot is reached wide enough to turn about, and then to set one's face toward the reaches of the sky and the open plain of the river.

The yellow sunset light steals like a golden dust through the aisles of the woods; the broad leaves of vines and bushes shine with a transparent glow like a hand held before a

candle, and the straight trunks of the trees are powdered with gold toward the west. The green light under the crowding branches begins to glitter as the level sunshine creeps like a rising tide among the bushes, and brims the cups of the Easter lilies with wonderful wine. The rustling "bonnets" are gilded until the whole creek seems to gleam and shimmer; and far away the St. John's reveals its placid expanse of gold against a golden sky, which has

not a cloud to blur its haze of glory. Just
as the creek, turning and hesitating around a
bank of lilies, is folded into the bosom of the
welcoming river, a fork-tailed kite springs suddenly up from among the leaves, and out across
the water. But save for the arrowy whir of its
flight, Night silently catches the drowsy earth in
a golden net, and draws it down among the stars.

Later, the twilight glimmers along low shores,
where orange-orchards stretch, dark and still,
across the level land. Under their branches
even at dusk the deep sand is warm from a day
of blazing sunshine; there is no grass about
their roots, only the hot red of flowering sorrel,
or some tufted weeds, with yellow blossoms. In
the deep green of the leaves, oranges shine like
lanterns, and blossoms glimmer with pale light;
but the branches are so thick that the air scarcely
stirs under them, and the perfume is overpowering. Sometimes a wandering breeze bears this
fragrance out upon the river; it is as thick and
palpable, almost, as the creamy flower itself.
The stars seem drunk with it, they shine with
such wonderful brightness.

Here and there, set in the green darkness of these orchards along the shore, one can see the white pillars of a broad veranda, and a great stack of chimneys above some square roof, or,

perhaps, crumbling wharves which reach far out into the river, and distant rows of cabins that were once "quarters," and resounded with laughter and the twang of the banjo and the jolly scuffle of dancing feet. Often they are deserted, these old stately houses; but where

they are occupied, there are open doors.   The
wayfaring man and those that travel in compa-
nies are received with so wide a hospitality that
its limits and boundaries cannot be seen.

In the falling dusk, one leaves the wash and
flow of the great river, and comes, through
myrtle-walks, through folding fragrance of
orange-orchards, through deepening shadows
under the live-oaks, up to such a doorway,
to learn much of the graciousness of Southern
hospitality.

THE END.